DISTRAUGHT
AND
DESTRUCTIVE

The (Sort of) Middle

MAPLE'S FANTASTIC STORIES

Book Two

By the Mighty and
Awesome Maple Twiggs

ISBN: 978-1-952065-04-0

First edition.

Maple Twiggs Publishing.

I see you there, eating your lunch alone.

This book is for you.

CONTENTS

CHAPTER ONE.

At Dinner.

A Weird Assortment of People and Furry Things.

Still Presented by Stella.

A Girl With Many Regrets.

Dinner was ready.

But I wasn't.

I had slipped back into the bathroom to stare at me and my new tattoos. For a few quiet moments. Before my father would inevitably yell at me to come eat.

<u>In Which Stella Speaks With the Author Whose Head She Lives Inside Of:</u>

(Stella: Maple, why did you do this to me?

Maple: Do what?

Stella: These tattoos!!! How can I ever go out into public again?!

Maple: Who said you were going out into public again?

Stella: Uh.

Maple: You could be killed in the next chapter.

Stella: Uh. But I'm the main character.

Maple: Oh, good. I'm glad you've finally accepted your fate as the main protagonist!

Stella: But why the need for 700 tattoos?!?!

Maple: Well, you have to stand out.

Stella: No, I don't.

Maple: Yes, you do.

Stella: Can't I just hide in this bathroom for the rest of the books?)

"Stellllaaaaaa!!!! Dinner is on the table!!!" my father bellowed.

I guess I can't hide in the bathroom for the rest of these books.

And I guess the fact that we were in someone else's house didn't stop him from bellowing.

I loped out of the bathroom. Into the kitchen. And slid into the empty chair next to my Dad. I pulled my hoodie's sleeves down over my forearms and wrists, hiding the most visible tattoos.

Pu, the magical cat who wears pink under-wear on his head, was seated on the other side of my father. I watched as he sneakily dropped ketchup-covered tater tots into my father's lap.

My father was unaware that this potato guer-illa warfare was occurring. I was aware that his pants could probably not be saved from the growing tomatoey stain.

Penny was passing dishes full of food up the table. And down the table. And back again. In an obvious-anxiety-induced panic that every-one should absolutely get enough food on their plates and in their mouths.

Probably so that no one would talk.

The three Demington sisters were staring at me. Chewing their food slowly. But never taking their eyes off me.

Archie, the other cat, was slathering butter-milk biscuits the size of his head with enough jam to cover a football field. And then devouring them. Slowly. In cat-size bites. He made eye con-tact with no one. Only having eyes for the bis-cuits and jam.

Eagle, the weird-looking rabbit, sighed heav-ily while looking at me, then my Dad, then

3

Penny, and then back to me. Then he stood up on the table, and jumped up and down on a bottle of maple syrup in order to squirt it all over the giant stack of pancakes on his plate.

Yes, we were having breakfast for dinner.

Which had been my unvoiced desire in the last book. And which these Demington girls had produced. I'm not sure how that had happened though. Could they read minds?

Wait, could *I read minds*?

What were the Godkiller's powers exactly?

And what were a lejerdemani's powers?

On our way to LAX, as we fled the state of California, my father had admitted that he was once a lejerdemani.

"So does this mean that Mom was a lejerdemani, too?" I asked him now, at this odd dinner.

"Let me think about that," he said and then he shoved a spoonful of scrambled eggs into his face.

'Let me think about that.'

Really?

Like I was asking for a favor.

Like he needed time to come up with an elaborate lie, when clearly the lies weren't cutting it anymore.

So I looked at Archie.

"Um," he said, and then stared at his biscuits.

So I went back to staring at my Dad, waiting for him to crack.

He never did.

But I did have other possible informants. So I looked at Penny.

Penny looked at my Dad. He looked at Penny. He fake-coughed.

"*Yeeeeessssssssssss*! She was," Pu said, as he threw Eagle's syrupy pile of pancakes into my Dad's face. With a quick magical movement of his paw. Pu never touched the pancakes. They just flew through the air with the greatest of ease.

I was going to have to get used to this.

My father started wiping the syrup off his face with Pu. As if he were a towel.

A claws-out fight erupted that resulted in my father standing up, thus dumping a pile of ketchupy tater tots onto his shoes and the floor.

"*What the?!?!*" he gasped.

Pu took the opportunity to try and kick his way out of my father's hands. But that didn't work.

The fight rolled into the hallway and then

the bathroom. For some more hissing and a de-syruping. I assume.

I looked at Penny.

She quickly went back to serving spoonfuls of tater tots onto Morrow's plate. Which already had a huge pile of tots on it.

Morrow looked at her like she was a nutter. Clearly no one was sane at this table though.

Well, that conversation attempt was a failure.

I went to reach for my fork and my new brace-let slid out from my sleeve. The Demingtons looked at it with marked curiosity.

I put my hands back in my lap.

I didn't really feel like eating anyway.

Instead I'll just nervously spin the bracelet around my wrist. Counting the rotations.

So if my mother was a lejerdemani, she had a signature metal, too, right? I wonder what kind? And I wonder what her signature pigment was? And she had a shadow creature like Pu, right? I wonder what he was? I wonder what my shadow creature would've been? If I had one.

Why was I thinking about all of this right now?

Okay. There's avocado on your plate, Stella.

At least pick up your fork and eat that.

"So have you always been a cat?" Morrow

asked Archie.

"Uhhh," he began.

"Good question," Nora interrupted. "A cat as the God of Destruction is sort of appropriate. But it's not the format I would've guessed."

"No. I haven't always been a cat. I'm usually in the form of a humanesque male," he answered, half-smiling shyly.

The conversation continued.

But I wasn't following it anymore.

I'm pretty sure I just blacked out as a piece of avocado dropped off my fork and back onto my plate. As my mouth hung open. And my eyes glazed over.

A humanesque male?

He meant a guy—right?

He was actually *a guy*—right???

Ssssshhhhhhiiiiii-.

I had just spent the last 24-some-odd-hours trying to pet his kitty belly fluff.

And he had spent those same 24-some-odd-hours trying to avoid me petting his kitty belly fluff.

And now I understood why.

Now I just seemed like a perverted lecherous psycho.

Also—he'd been in the bathroom the whole time I was showering all that marble dust off of me.

God. No.

Also—he'd seen me pack all of my underwear, bras, and girl-related supplies into my suitcase.

God. No.

And—he'd watched me brush my teeth, spit into the sink, wash my face, and pick at zits on my nose for like 30 minutes before we left the house for the airport.

God. No.

And—I had held him in my lap during the whole flight.

God. No.

And—he was actually a dude. Like a human-esque dude.

God. No.

Imagine your family Fido suddenly turning into a full-grown male human thing and saying: "Yes, I've seen everything you've done. Ever."

God. No.

Please tell me this guy gets amnesia. Please???

"Have you ever tried throwing yourself against a wall? Or having someone else throw you up against a wall?" Nora asked Archie.

"What's wrong with you?" Ellie asked her.

"No, listen. Ellie, you told me about this yourself. In the original telling of 'The Princess and the Frog,' the frog gets thrown up against a wall and that's when he turns back into the prince-slash-attractive male character. It didn't have anything to do with a kiss or romance or love or anything. It was just blatant violence that solved the issue," Nora explained.

"I don't think that particular approach will turn Archie back into his male human form," Penny said and then sighed.

"No, it probably won't," _the cat who was really a damn man_ said. "I'll figure it all out at some point though. So don't worry about me."

No.

I am worried about you.

Really, really, _really_ worried about you.

Maybe you can just stay as a cat forever and then I'd never have to live through the embarrassment of seeing the man that I held in my lap for that whole flight? Was that too much to ask for???

Not only did I have to accept the fact that Pu had been living inside my head for most of my life, now I had to deal with this.

Was my existence based purely upon misery?

<u>In Which Stella Speaks Again With the Author
Whose Head She Lives Inside Of:</u>

(Stella: You're enjoying this. Aren't you,
Maple?

Maple: Maybe a little.

Stella: You told me that Archie is my love
interest. And I assumed he'd be a man. Then later
you introduce him as a cat. Which confused the
royal poo out of me. *THEN* you tell me *he's really
a man-dude-guy-thing*, after I treated him like a
damn cat for like a whole day. Why? Why are you
torturing me? Do I really end up with a man or
do I end up with a cat?? Just tell me now so I can
accept my fate.

Maple: If I tell you now it'll ruin some of my
fun!

Stella: Well. Well, as long as we don't ruin *your*
fun.

Maple: I'm glad you understand that this is
really all about me.)

"I'll throw you up against a wall if you want to
try that," Pu suggested as he returned from the

de-syruping.

"No, thanks," Archie replied.

"So does everyone know that Stella held Archie in her lap for the *whole flight*?!?" Pu asked, super-loudly, while grinning. "And does everyone know how awkward that'll be later???"

Oh. Yeah.

Pu was there for that, too.

All of that.

Aggcckkhhhsshhhh.

"I've heard the author say they end up together," Pu whispered.

"Whooaaaa," Nora said as her sisters covered their mouths in shock.

"No, no, no, no," I said as I shook my hands in the air. "That's a misunderstanding."

Meanwhile Archie was choking on a fried egg. Or a hairball. Or just pretending to, so he didn't have to talk or look at me.

"Do you think it's true that you end up with Stella???" Nora asked Archie.

Despite the fact that he clearly didn't want to engage in this conversation.

"I probably have too much baggage to be with anyone," he replied after he finished fake-choking.

What does that mean?

"There isn't a person alive without baggage," Eagle said. "We just have to learn how to function with the emotional dump of problems we all carry around in our pants."

"Uhhhhhh, we're trying to eat here, Eagle," Penny interrupted.

"What are we talking about?" my father asked as he entered the kitchen.

"How Stella and Archie are destined to be a couple," Pu said.

My father glared at me.

As if I had something to do with all of this.

Then he wiped off his ketchupy chair with some napkins and sat down.

"That's absurd," he said. "We don't need your jokes right now, Pu."

"What *do* you need then, Sweetie? S'more tater tots?" Pu asked, with fake saccharine innocence and a wink.

"I need to know what's *actually* going on here," my father hissed, as he shifted his glare to Archie. "This is a very nice distracting dinner and everything—but how do we hide from Verbena now that Pu is released? Will Penny's force field be enough?"

Archie kitty-smiled uncomfortably, while looking at the abrasive man.

"I assume she still wants to kill Stella," my father continued. "And probably the rest of us. And what was up with that die earlier in the bedroom, cat-god?"

Profound bitterness oozed from his voice.

"Well, you weren't really hiding from Verbena," Archie said.

"Huh?" my father asked.

"That was Riot, a God of Death, in uh, Verbena's body. You were hiding from Riot."

Penny stared at the cat-god, her mouth hanging open, as tears welled-up in her eyes.

"Verbena's body? Verbena isn't Verbena?" she asked him.

"No, Verbena is dead. And Riot took over her body to use it. Probably to avoid the Lastangs," Archie replied as he itched his nose.

An awkward silence descended upon the group.

Everyone stopped chewing and gave each other side-glances as Penny stared at her plate of food with wide eyes.

"So she's gone?" Eagle asked.

"Yes," Archie replied.

"*Gone?!*" my father spat.

"Yes," Archie repeated, more softly.

"*And the die? What's that about?!*" my father yelled, his face becoming noticeably redder as the seconds ticked by.

"It's about the current Godkiller. She's trapped inside a game. Courtesy of Riot. Well, really she's inside a painting, inside a game, that is connected to that die and that robot. Sylvie has to train Stella so that she can kill Riot. But first we have to find Sylvie. I can sense her blood aura from the robot, so I think she sent him here with that die. And that's probably why the die gave Stella migraines. Because it needs her."

My father stared at the cat-god with wide eyes.

I stared at everyone in turn with wide-eyes.

This was becoming a very wide-eyed meal.

"I have to kill someone?" I asked.

"No you don't," my father barked.

Archie had opened his tiny kitty mouth to speak, but then shut it again.

But he stared at me and I stared back at him.

And his cat eyeballs said: 'Yes, you have to kill someone.'

"We don't even know if she's really the Godkiller," my father said.

"Look at her Derek. What else could she be?" Penny asked quietly.

"Well, still. Whatever. Sylvie can kill Riot," my father replied.

"She may no longer have the ability to accomplish that," Archie half-whispered.

So I'm gonna have to kill someone.

Right?

Can't we just say all this clearly?

And who is Verbena?

I can't ask that now though.

"What's this game you're talking about?" Morrow asked Archie.

Thank goodness someone else was willing to ask questions.

"The Game of Goose. It's sort of connected to my Realm of Destruction, the House of Coventry," Archie said.

Penny dropped her fork down onto her plate. The clatter stunned all of us for a moment. Then she looked at Archie and crossed her arms.

"Can you go back to the beginning and explain what's really going on?" Penny asked through her now-obvious tears.

I guess she could finally vocalize her thoughts.

"Well…" he began.

"I mean, who are we really up against here? Who's the villain? And what's been going on all these years?" she asked. "Do you even know??"

AN
INTERRUPTION.

By Maple, the Magnificent Author of this Amazing Story.

(Maple: I'm gonna need everyone to pull together for this part. Who wants to explain who the villain is in this tale?

Archie: It's me. So I should explain.

Sylvie: Uh, no it's me. I should explain.

Riot: It's definitely not me. Don't look at me to explain. I didn't do anything wrong.

Maple: How is that possible? You killed a bunch of people. Like a big bunch of people.

Riot: So? I'm a God of Death. That's my job.

Maple: But. It wasn't…well. Okay, okay. Clearly we need to work on this step by step. We'll start with Sylvie. Deliberate on the past and on the nature of evil. Go.)

CHAPTER TWO.

I Am Sylvie.

Unfortunately.

(Sylvie: I'm supposed to do what? Deliberate on what?

Maple: The past and evil.

Sylvie: The what?

Maple: Just tell your story. Don't think too hard. I know you're going through a lot right now.

Sylvie: I *am* going through a lot right now. But you want me to write some abstruse part of your book for you? I'm stuck in bed, in pain, and barely able to move. And you want me to do something? How does that make sense?

Maple: It makes sense to me.

Sylvie: Ughck. So what do I talk about again?

Maple: Your life story.

Sylvie: *My whole life story?!*

Maple: Yes.

Sylvie: Are you insane? Do you know how long I've been alive? And do you know how many painkillers I'm on right now? How do you expect me to be lucid?

Stella: Why are we making this ill woman talk? Or rather, write?

Maple: Well, she's got to explain how she came to be stuck inside a lost Frida Kahlo painting.

Sylvie: I do?

Maple: Yeah. That way we know about the past horrendous mess that led to Stella being in the current horrendous mess.

Stella: I'm in a horrendous mess?

Maple: Of course you are.

Stella: ...)

Well. Uh. I am Sylvie. Unfortunately.

And I am the Godkiller. Sort Of. Unfortunately.

And I probably made this horrendous mess. Unfortunately.

I have often wondered who the real villain is in this tale.

It's probably me.

Me because of my cowardice. My inability to

make decisions. My refusal to take on real responsibility.

I spent my whole life lost in my own mind, refusing to come out of it. And there were consequences. Dire consequences.

So I'm the villain. Although I didn't kill anyone.

And that's the problem. I didn't kill anyone, when I should have.

And now I'm trapped.

Stuck.

And in pain.

(Maple: You seem really focused on your pain right now.

Sylvie: That's because I'm in pain.

Maple: Physical and mental?

Sylvie: Yes.

Maple: Hmmm. Maybe we can address your emotional pain at least. My cognitive behavioral therapist recommends writing letters to express your feelings. So write a letter to the person you most want to talk to in this moment.

Sylvie: Are you kidding?

Maple: No. I can't help you if you aren't willing to help yourself.

Sylvie: You are ridiculous.
Maple: Go on.)

I slowly sat up in my bed, pushing myself up one inch at a time. And then I pulled my tray table over my lap. I shuffled through my notes to find a blank piece of paper. Then I fumbled to grip a pen to write the first word.

D e a r

There. You can do it Sylvie. Keep going.

Dear Ozzie,

I know I made some mistakes. But I thought what we had together was bigger than our missteps, bigger than our differences.

I thought it meant more. I thought we were us. I thought I was enough for you.

You were enough for me.

Don't you want to see me again? Or have you abandoned me here?

Where are you? And why haven't you come to get me?

Were we ever really in love?

How exactly do you feel?

With Love, From Me

I crinkled up the note and threw it across the room. I don't think this form of therapy is helping. It's just making me think about things that will make me cry. I need to stop listening to the author.

I pushed the tray table off my lap, and onto the floor. Papers and pens scattered.

Then I tried to shift my weight back down further into the bed, but I couldn't move. I had used up all of my energy sitting up and writing that stupid letter.

"Why are you making a racket in here *now*?!" Sapo-Rana asked as he flew into the room.

I stared at the dove, but didn't reply.

How do I explain about my conversation with the author and my letter to Ozzie?

A letter that sounded like desperate, immature begging.

And an author who just sounded immature.

So I sighed instead.

"Uh, what's wrong with you? Did you take your pills? *How many* did you take?" he asked, narrowing his gaze.

I stared at the dove, but still didn't reply.

How many pills had I taken?

I don't know. I can't remember.

"I'm going to get Paloma," he said as he flew back out of the room.

I sighed again, more heavily this time.

(Maple: You know, this story isn't going to tell itself. Keep it moving.

Sylvie: But I don't even have anyone to explain it to now. I'm alone in this room, once again.

Maple: Make it work.)

I began tapping the floral decorations on the quilt draped over my semi-paralyzed body. They sprouted up from the fabric as real flowers, creating a garden across my lap.

Does it even matter if anyone is here?

I'll just talk to my flowers.

"I was kidnapped. It wasn't an actual 'bag-over-the-head-chloroform-over-the-mouth' kidnapping," I said.

I touched one poppy and one daisy.

They grew legs and stepped out of my quilt.

Then they performed a silent pantomime of the poppy kidnapping the daisy.

Dang. I should've made these things into magical mime flowers a long time ago.

"I was tricked into going into this painting," I

continued. "And I can't get out of it. So I'm stuck here. And I've been stuck here for a very long time and now I'm dying."

The poppy and daisy then took turns performing dramatic death scenes across my lap. Being strangled. Drowning. Having a heart attack.

Sapo-Rana and Paloma were really missing out. This was great stuff. Although I do wonder, did I really make these mime flowers or was I just hallucinating them??

"But anyway. Where was I? Oh, yes. One could argue that the real villain of this tale is the woman who trapped me in this painting. Well, technically she's a god, not just a woman. But I'm my own worst enemy, because if I had just killed her—I wouldn't be in this painting."

The poppy and daisy nodded, wordlessly acknowledging me.

At least I had them.

In some ways it's quite ironic, or perhaps just fitting, that I will end my life trapped in something. As I began my life trapped in something. During my time with Old Kunkerpot and the Four Dogs of the Apocalypse, as I called them. Although I didn't realize I was trapped. I just believed I was being protected. I guess you could say it was both.

In my current situation I've often thought about these questions:

When is a paradise a prison?

And when is a prison a paradise?

I grew up in a lovely house, with a lovely yard, surrounded by seven lovely trees that talked with me and entertained me during my many hours playing outside. That was my whole world. The four dogs, Muddiford, Wooferton, Cadby, and Beamish, cooked, cleaned, and gave me my lessons.

The fact that they could talk and walk like me didn't seem odd, as that's what I grew up with. It was only later in life that I learned that dogs typically don't spend their days dusting the knick-knacks and lecturing children on keeping their elbows off the table.

Old Kunkerpot, my guardian, only appeared when he needed to administer tests of my abilities. Again, it was only later in life that I learned what he spent his days doing out there in the other Realms. And it was only later in life that I learned that he had stolen me from my parents, and trapped me in this Realm of his own creation.

But as far back as I can remember, I always knew why my four dogs were teaching me magic, and why Old Kunkerpot kept testing me. Slowly I was inheriting his abilities. And when he was dead it would be my turn to kill those who needed killing.

"Unfortunately, no one ever tested whether or not I could actually kill. Whether or not I could do the job when face to face with my mark," I said out loud, to my flowers.

The poppy and the daisy exchanged a glance, and shrugged.

"But the opportunity to test me in this regard arrived at our doorstep one day...."

Insert thick misty fog for an emotional flashback to many years ago

"Huckle Buckle Bean Stalk!" the new voice called out.

"That's not Old Kunkerpot," Muddiford said, standing next to the door and sniffing the air.

"He hasn't been by for a whole week. That's not like him. Maybe he sent somebody else as a messenger. Maybe something is wrong," Cadby said.

"Why would he send somebody else? That's

nutty. That's against our whole system," Wooferton replied.

"Huckle Buckle Bean Stalk!" the voice called out again.

Meanwhile, Beamish was squirming by the door.

You see, Beamish was obsessed with games. And Old Kunkerpot and Beamish had established this call-and-response game where Old Kunkerpot would yell out 'huckle buckle bean stalk' upon his arrival, and Beamish would reply with 'hot boiled beans and butter; walk in and find your supper!' And the front door would unlock and in would walk Old Kunkerpot.

So all Beamish, who really wasn't the brightest bulb in the box, wanted to do was reply with his 'hot boiled beans' refrain.

His squirming intensified as the voice called out a third time: "Huckle Buckle Bean Stalk!"

"Don't you dare," Cadby said to Beamish.

He was the first to realize what he was about to do.

But that came too late.

"Hot boiled beans and butter; walk in and find your supper!" Beamish called out to the stranger.

My stomach dropped.

I had been sitting at the kitchen table, working on my lessons.

But now this was a crisis. My normal little life would no longer be normal. Or rather, I would soon discover that I never had a normal little life.

"Sonova!!!" Muddiford shouted as he reached to put his paw over Beamish's mouth.

The front door opened and in walked a woman with snakes for hair.

As she cheerfully said: "Hello puppies!" she looked at my four dogs and turned them to stone.

My breathing faltered.

"*Hiltzen!*" I screamed as I stood up from my chair and cast a death spell onto the woman.

But she disappeared.

Well, she didn't quite disappear. She was zapped into a shield that was being held by a young man who stood in my doorway.

The young man who had been calling out: "Huckle Buckle Bean Stalk."

The young man who I wanted to grab by the throat and throttle.

"I thought you would be a child," he said to me, his face full of more surprise than mine was.

"I am a child," I replied.

"No, you aren't. You're a woman."

"I'm only eighteen years old. I'm a child."

"No, that's a woman."

I rolled my eyes at him.

"Who are you and what have you done to my dogs?!"

"I'm sorry. I was pretty sure you'd be a child," he continued, ignoring my questions.

I walked over to Wooferton and placed my hand upon the cold stone statue. I began casting spells in my head to reverse whatever the snake-haired woman had done.

"No, no. Don't do that," the young man said.

"Should I kill you first and then fix them?" I asked, bitterly. "They are fix-able, correct?"

"Yes, I mean—Medusa can fix them. But only after you answer a question for me."

"And what is that question?" I asked, crossing my arms.

"Where's the Jainkohiltzaile?"

"He's out."

"I see."

I stared at him with a look of disgust oozing off my face.

"You must have followed him here before to

learn about the Huckle Buckle Bean Stalk thing, so I'm not sure why you're asking me where he is. You go out there and find him. *After* you fix my dogs."

"You're too old," he said, staring back at me, seemingly ignoring everything I had just said.

"Thank you? Thank you so much."

"No. You should be a child. A child without— without…."

"Without the powers of the Jainkohiltzaile?"

"Yes. That's what I'm thinking."

"I don't have the full powers of the Jainkohiltzaile," I replied. "But if you came here to kill me I will put up quite a fight. You will have to bring out more than a Medusa."

"You do have the full powers. I can sense them. And I no longer have the ability to kill you. But you can certainly kill me."

I slowly understood what he was saying. If I had the full powers, then the old Jainkohiltzaile was dead and the transfer was complete. I was now the Godkiller. And Old Kunkerpot was dead.

"Fix. My. Dogs," I commanded.

"Medusa?" the young man called out.

She zapped out of the shield in front of me.

"Sorry poppet," she said. "But you didn't have to try and kill me. We were only coming to rescue you."

"Rescue me?"

"Well, we weren't actually coming to rescue her, Medusa. That was a lie," the young man said, chuckling in a weird way. "I was sent to kill her. But I can't do that now."

"Kill her? Oh no. I don't want any part of that!" she announced as she quickly touched each of my dogs and turned them back into dogs. "Don't call on me for awhile, Ozzie. I'm mad at you."

And in she went, back into the shield. Pouting and scowling.

The young man, who was apparently called Ozzie, put the shield down as my four dogs confronted him.

"He's a God of Death, Sylvie! How'd he get in here?!?!" Muddiford gasped.

"Beamish let him in," I replied.

Everyone glared at Beamish, who shrugged.

"Old Kunkerpot is dead, and I'm the full Jainkohiltzaile," I said. "He was sent to kill me, but he can't now."

Everyone turned to glare at Ozzie, who shrugged.

"I accept my fate," he said and then smiled at me.

"You were going to kill me, and now you're smiling at me?" I asked in disbelief.

"Well, to be honest you would've been the first thing I've ever killed, so it's not like I know what I'm doing," he replied.

"Kill him," Wooferton said. "Kill him and send a message to the gods. Then they'll know not to send anybody else for you."

I looked at Wooferton, acknowledging the command.

Then I looked at Ozzie. But my blood thirst was gone. The man who I had wanted to choke to death was no longer in front of me. He was just a naïve young man, waiting for his destiny to play out.

It was at that moment that I began to ponder things that I was never meant to ponder. I questioned the need for the existence of a Jainkohilt-zaile. What was the point? Did I have to kill this God of Death just to send a message?

He was like me—destined to kill things but never having killed anything before. How does one cross that line? How does one make that mental commitment? You can never go back to not being a murderer.

If I am the Godkiller, am I a murderer? Or am I just the executor of justice? But how could killing this god be justice?

I wouldn't be able to die for another thousand years. So whoever and whatever they sent wouldn't be able to kill me until that time. Just like Old Kunkerpot, I would simply live as long as I was meant to.

Was there a point to me killing this Ozzie? It seemed like a waste of his life. He was just a terrible assassin. Did he deserve to die? Perhaps I just felt sorry for him. Perhaps I just felt sorry for myself.

"Go on, kill him," Muddiford said. "This is the moment we've been training for your whole life."

That's when it struck me.

The thing I had spent my whole life training to do seemed pointless and meaningless and a waste. And I didn't want to do it. Perhaps killing this god was the responsible thing to do. But I was still just a child, at least in my mind, and I wasn't going to kill him.

"Do you want to play the Game of Goose?" I asked him, instead.

Cough.

Who was coughing?

Cough.

It was Sapo-Rana coughing into my face.

I had closed my eyes and hadn't noticed that he had perched himself on top of my head. He had returned to my room with his toad companion, Paloma.

"Did you really just tell that whole story as a monologue to this empty room???" he asked me.

"Did I say all of that out loud?" I asked.

"I think you did, sweetie," Paloma said.

"Oh. I didn't realize that."

"Who are you talking to???" Sapo-Rana pushed.

"Uh. I don't know. But I think the flowers were listening."

CHAPTER THREE.

*In Which We Travel Much Further
Back in Time to the Point Where Riot
Is Brought Into This Plot.*

By Riot.

(Maple: Okay. Riot, it's your turn.

Riot: My turn for what?

Maple: To talk about the origins of the horrendous mess.

Riot: I don't want to.

Maple: You have to. The people have to know what you did.

Riot: What people? I'm a god. They don't deserve to know what I did.

Maple: Do you want someone else to explain your side of the story?

Riot: No! How dare they!

Maple: So, go on. I'll give you a gold star sticker and a check mark on your official record when you're done.

Riot: Oh. Well, in that case I should get started.)

"Oh, Riot!" Tiziano called to me in his annoying singsong voice from outside my office door.

"The door's closed for a reason, Tiziano. Come back later. I'm trying to finish my paperwork," I responded.

He burst through my closed door anyway.

Surprise, surprise.

"You'll *never* guess the report I've just received," he said, grinning at me with an evil glint in his eye.

"What?" I asked. "What is it now?"

"You know that assignment your brother Ozzie was sent off on? Well, a little birdie told me what it was."

"And?"

"He was sent to kill the next Jainkohiltzaile."

His smile became even wider as I stood up from my chair.

"He was what?" I asked.

"The next Jainkohiltzaile. He was sent to kill

her before the current Jainkohiltzaile kicked it. But he was too late, and she was already 100% the Jainkohiltzaile."

"Is he dead? *Did she kill him?!?*"

"Nope. Apparently they've become fast friends and they spend their days together goofing off with Archie."

"Archie?"

"Suntsitzea. The God of Destruction. Remember him? Your brother's BFF-slash-bromance-dude?"

"Oh yes, right. Him."

"And the word on the street is that Ozzie and the Jainkohiltzaile are quite close. Like *quite* close. And another little birdie told me that *you're* gonna get in trouble for his screw-up."

"Shouldn't you have started this conversation with that piece of information?"

Seconds later....

"*Riot! Riot!*"

That was my boss, the Regional Manager.

"Riot!"

"Yes?"

"Your brother messed up big! He can't even kill a single young girl! He was the top of his class, and now he's completely useless! So disappointing. *You're* gonna have to figure out who the next Jainkohiltzaile is and kill them before he or she can get those powers," he explained brusquely—while shaking his finger at me the whole time.

"Just *why* are we doing that again?" I asked, scratching my head.

"It's the orders from above," he replied.

'Above' most likely referred to the Four Gods of the Apocalypse, the gods who were the bosses of our bosses of our bosses—and the creators of all of the Gods of Death. Who were just little pissants like my brother and me, and even the Regional Manager. We were all just worthless little cogs in the machine.

The Four Gods of the Apocalypse are the gods of Famine, Pestilence, Disease, and War. They were formerly known collectively as the 'Gods of Death.' But when they read about the impressive name of the 'Four Horsemen of the Apocalypse' in the *Book of Revelation*, they decided to adapt their name so it would sound more striking. These four gods are the parents of all of the Gods of Death, including Ozzie and me.

As the Regional Manager glared at me, my overwhelming and nearly-paralyzing sense of duty told me to go check on my brother and attempt to carry out the task placed upon me. Despite the fact that I was just a lowly pissant.

But how do I 'figure out who the next Jainkohiltzaile is and kill them before he or she can get those powers?' How's that even possible when he or she won't be born for another several hundred years?

Sure, you can track them down after they've been born—usually. But if they aren't alive yet? How is that possible?

"Yes, sir," I said as I nodded at the Regional Manager, who then stormed out of my office.

"Oh, the burden of siblings," Tiziano sang as he darted away, clearly trying to avoid any task I was going to assign him so that he could actually help me, like he was supposed to.

I stared at the perpetual paperwork on my desk, but my thoughts drifted to Ozzie. What exactly was he up to now?

Being only two years younger than me, we'd gone to school together. Although we hadn't been in the same classes, I'd kept an eye on him.

I had many other brothers and sisters. Thousands, in fact. As the human population increased the demand for Gods of Death increased.

So more of us were born to balance out the workload of killing off the humans.

When it was their time, of course.

But while there were thousands of Gods of Death, there was only one Ozzie in my heart. Only one little brother that I cared for. And only one little brother that I felt the need to clean up after his mess.

Which is what I now had to do.

I found Ozzie, Archie, and the Jainkohiltzaile on an island off the coast of Italy. Lounging on a sun-drenched balcony. Enjoying a resplendent breakfast.

I stared at the three of them from a distance.

They seemed happy enough.

The Jainkohiltzaile was a woman, this time. Well, a girl really. A young woman? I'm not sure how to label her. She was smiling at my brother Ozzie, who was smiling back. And the third person was Archie, who was savoring some sort of jam-covered breakfast treat.

Archie.

I had heard that name many times from my brother, but I had never met him face to face. They had been in the same classes at school, even though Archie didn't really need to go to school. Since he was much older than all of us. But apparently he kept going to classes just for fun.

Archie.

He was stunning. My mind went fuzzy just watching him. And I couldn't stop staring at him. His beauty, or handsomeness, or presence, or something was almost enough to make me forget why I had shown up here.

But I had come to assess the situation and come up with a plan. So I needed to do that. This meant actually approaching them though, and I was finding it difficult to move my legs in their direction.

Just then Ischia, Tiziano's sister, came up behind me and nudged me forward.

"Tiziano told me you got a job. So I'm here to help," she announced. "Does the job involve talking to the hunky Suntsitzea over there?"

She started to drool a little.

"Well, yes, in a way. We have to talk to all of them. But in a subtle manner."

"Subtle is my middle name!" she replied.

It was indeed *not* her middle name.

"Ozzie!!!!" she shouted to them, as she strode

41

across the plaza toward the balcony of romantic breakfasts.

Ischia and Tiziano were my demi-gods: half-gods assigned to assist me in my duties. But honestly, it felt more like they were assigned to hinder me in my duties. I spent more time managing them than actually accomplishing anything.

"Ozzie!!!" Ischia called out again, making sure everyone noticed us.

I hadn't even come up with a plan on how to talk in front of Archie yet. I couldn't even imagine looking at him more closely. But I followed after Ischia just the same. God only knows what she'd do without me standing next to her.

As we approached the table I could see Ozzie's face getting more and more pale.

"Riot," he said, standing up. "Uh. This is Sylvie, and this is Archie. Guys, this is my sister, Riot."

"And I'm Ischia," she said, shaking Archie's hand with a sort of groping-like-level of affection.

"And that's Ischia," Ozzie added as he pointed to her.

I shook Sylvie and Archie's hand. But sort of numbly. Nodding the whole time like a dumb puppet on a string.

"Would you like to join us for the Game of Goose?" Archie asked me, smiling.

Asked me. Smiling. At me.

"We're going to start playing right after breakfast. Would you like some breakfast?" he continued.

Those big brown eyes kept smiling at me. And I couldn't say no.

So Ischia and I had breakfast with them. And we began to play the Game of Goose with them. Well, their version of the Game of Goose. Which was the kind of pointless amusement that only people with too much time on their hands would invent.

Ischia kept trying to walk arm in arm with Archie.

And I kept pulling her off of him.

She kept talking with him.

And I kept staring at him.

Ozzie would look at me, sheepishly.

Sylvie would smile at me, innocently.

For now, I allowed myself to get lost in their world.

Or at least I pretended to get lost.

I wasn't interested in blatantly giving Sylvie a reason to kill me. She was the Jainkohiltzaile after all. The only being alive that could kill a god. And I just happened to be a god.

But as we spent the rest of the day—and then the rest of the week—playing that inane Game of Goose, in the back of my mind I knew that my brother had failed the Four Gods of the Apocalypse.

And that they would not happily accept it if I did the same.

One day, Archie, Ischia, Sylvie, Ozzie, and I (say that ten times fast) were in a landscape painting trying to catch a runaway coach for the stupid Game of Goose.

It was then, as I watched the wheels of the coach race by, that I realized what being a fifth-wheel felt like. They were all giggling like morons while Ozzie attempted to mount a horse—in order to chase after the coach. But he was failing miserably.

Which they thought was hilarious.

And I regarded as pointless.

It had been months, if not years, of us play-ing this game and goofing off. Ischia and Archie were always together, although he never really seemed interested in her romantically.

But clearly he wasn't interested in me romantically either.

My life just kept spinning and spinning and spinning like those coach wheels. Going and going, but going nowhere.

Meanwhile, Ozzie and Sylvie were growing closer every day.

Watching them I learned several things:

1) She probably wasn't going to kill my brother.

2) She probably wasn't going to kill me.

3) Despite the fact that she seemed completely capable, she wasn't going to kill any gods.

And this last piece of knowledge confused me greatly. Because that's what she had been born to do. A Jainkohiltzaile was supposed to kill gods. Any time one of us got out of hand, she was supposed to come in, mow him down, and a new god would be born in his place—fresh and new, and un-spoiled.

But Sylvie didn't seem interested in that job. She didn't seem interested in any job. She just wanted to hang out with my brother 24-7.

Which I admit, was becoming tiresome.

After I learned those first three things, I waited to see if Sylvie ever discussed the next Jainkohiltzaile. For example, was she going to train that person? The topic never came up. She knew her life was finite. She knew she only had 1,000 years of life. But that didn't seem to matter.

She never looked ahead. She never thought of the future. She never seemed to think about the world outside of this couple-hood she had created with Ozzie.

Which I admit, was also becoming tiresome.

I wasn't about to tell the woman to do her job, and kill some gods, and find the next Jainko-hiltzaile, and train him or her. That would be against my orders. And hence, against logic. If she remained useless that would certainly please my bosses. They didn't want her to do her job.

But recently there were many moments that I sat back and wondered: what *was* going on in her head?

And the answer that I landed upon was: there was nothing going on in her head.

Ozzie knew that I was frustrated with what was happening, but I never told him why I was really there. So he just kept trying to entertain and amuse me, thinking that would make up for him dating the Jainkohiltzaile.

But that behavior was also becoming tiresome.

He lacked the initiative to just tell me what had happened, and what was happening between Sylvie and him, and he avoided all conversation about the future.

And Ischia. Well, I was ready to throttle her, and most mornings I woke up thinking of ways to murder her. I had never been this possessive of a man before. But Archie was different. I eventually realized that *because* Archie was the God of Destruction he was destined to destroy relationships. As much as he could destroy buildings and cities and forests and mountains, he could also destroy lives. I don't think he ever realized that fact.

Well, maybe he did later.

But back to my discussion of Ischia: while once upon a time I could put up with her child-like, over-the-top antics, now they simply ticked me off.

And the fact that Archie just accepted all of her petting, groping flirtatiousness was infuriating. Not just tiresome. Infuriating.

If you don't like the girl just tell her you don't like her and stop allowing her to sit on your lap whenever she pleases.

He just acted like a rigid, unfeeling statue. Too polite and un-emotional to say or do anything. Did he even comprehend the concept of affection? Ischia was certainly doing her best to make him understand. That girl.

Was I mad at her? Or him? Or myself?

I had certainly made no movements toward him myself. And he had made no movements toward me.

So here we were. Trying to catch a stupid runaway coach. Accomplishing nothing. Day by day. Doing less and less.

And there was a point when I decided that I needed to do something.

But how did I kill the next Jainkohiltzaile if I didn't know who he or she was? And how would I make sure Ozzie, Sylvie, and even Archie didn't get in my way?

Clearly they appeared to be completely unmotivated to participate in the real world, but what would happen if they knew I was hunting the next Jainkohiltzaile? Would that mean something to them?

All of these questions were swirling around in my head the day I met Horace Welser. And he provided me with many of the answers I was seeking.

It was the day we needed to find the ghost of Salvador Dalí's childhood pet bat in the Realm of the Dead.

Yes, you read that right—a dead pet bat.

And yes, this was for that idiotic Game of Goose.

If you haven't caught on by now, the Game simultaneously exists in all times and in no time. So yes, we could meet the ghost of Cimabue, Dalí, Gentileschi, or whoever, whenever we rolled the dice.

The game was in its own mysterious sub-Realm. Supposedly it had been invented by Sylvie's mentor—whom she only referred to as 'Old Kunkerpot'—but Archie suspected that it had even earlier origins.

But. *Ugh*. This dumb game. Wait. Before I go off on a tirade about the game's maddening point-lessness, we should discuss Horace.

We called upon him late one afternoon at his cottage in the woods. He was a close lejerdemani friend of Archie's and had worked with him for years. Horace looked about 40 years old, but had already lived for hundreds of years. And probably would've lived for hundreds more years if I hadn't killed him.

That's one of the annoying things about lejerdemani—they can live way, way past the normal human lifespan. And that really messes up the algorithms for the Death Databases back at the office.

And in Horace's case, he was a bit of an inventor, a poker and prodder into things that he probably shouldn't have ever poked and prodded into. So he had figured out some magic that would increase his already-lengthened lejerdemani lifespan.

His incessant need to push the boundaries of magic proved useful to me.

For the pet bat issue he gave us an enhanced ancient Chinese lejerdemani geomancy board that would help us track it down and reunite it with its owner.

Sigh. So stupid.

But then I used this board to track down the ancestors of the next Jainkohiltzaile and kill that family. Of course, not while Archie, Ozzie, and Sylvie were around. That was just a job for Ischia and me.

However, then another family appeared on the board as the ancestors of the Jainkohiltzaile.

No matter how many families I killed, another one would show up on the board. And unfortunately, people started to notice that someone was showing up and murdering lejerdemani families out of the blue.

So I had to continue my work in disguise.

But how could I disguise myself most effectively?

It was at this point that I decided to befriend Horace. I kept visiting him now and again, seemingly there to ask questions related to the Game of Goose.

Meanwhile, he was seemingly ecstatic that someone was there who wanted to talk 'shop' with him, as his wife had little patience to listen to him drone on and on about his discoveries. But I listened and listened, taking mental notes along the way. And, much to his delight, I never seemed to tire of his droning on and on.

It was only once—just once, for a moment—that I felt a brief hint of sadness when I realized that he too would have to be murdered, and his whole family.

Because, as I eventually figured out, the only

guaranteed way to prevent another Jainkohilt-zaile from being born was to kill all of the lejer-demani.

(Riot: There I did it. I told my story. Where's my gold star sticker and check mark?

Maple: You only told part of it, you nincom-poop. You have to keep going.

Riot: No I don't. This was my whole story.

Maple: It really wasn't.

Riot: Well, I don't want to tell the rest.

Maple: If you do, I'll give you an official com-mendation marked down in the annals of the Office of Death.

Riot: Okay, but only if you give me that gold star sticker and check mark first.

Maple: Deal.)

CHAPTER FOUR.

Why You Shouldn't Write Things Down.

Written Down by Riot.

I turned my brother into a Boulle cabinet.

I guess really more of an armoire.

At nearly eight feet high, it towered over me. Suggesting it was more of an armoire than a cabinet....

I stood still staring at it for quite some time.

I was tempted to touch it, but then I realized I wouldn't know exactly what I was touching.

It was quite a nice armoire. Early 18th century. French. Once burnt to a crisp in the fire that swept through Boulle's apartment and workshops in the halls of the Louvre palace in 1720.

Then it showed up in the House of Coventry. And currently stood in one of Henry Coventry's sitting rooms.

It was made from a fine hard oak. Veneered with Macassar and Gabon ebony, fruitwood, and burl wood. Adorned with marquetry of tortoiseshell, copper, brass, and a delightful dark purple amaranth. It had gilt bronze mounts. The combination of the dark woods and the brilliant metals was striking. Flowery imagery of the wind gods spread across the front panels. Well, they can serve to keep Ozzie company.

This transformation was the moment of my fatal mistake. Well, truly, my fatal mistake was made several moments earlier. Although I suppose even that point could be argued.

****Insert obligatory flashback to several moments earlier****

"Riot!" Ozzie called to me from the sitting room around the corner. "Riot, this book here is screaming. Why's it doing that?"

Oh. Damn.

I had left my ledger on the side table in that very sitting room. The ledger in which I wrote down every name of every lejerdemani I had killed, or had had killed.

Why did I write all of that down like a giant

idiot? Well, I was trying to keep track of the names to guarantee my success on the Jainko-hiltzaile front, amongst other reasons.

I turned the corner to find him reading the 'screaming' ledger.

"That's mine," I said as I cast a spell to call the book to me.

But Ozzie countered my spell, blocked it successfully, and kept reading.

"Why do you have these names? And why is this screaming? These names..." he said as his voice drifted off.

He closed the ledger and looked at me.

"These are the names of the lejerdemani that have died over the past years. They were killed mysteriously, or under bizarre circumstances," he said, his gaze narrowing.

"I was just keeping track. So many of them have been dying, at a higher rate than normal, that I thought I needed to look into it," I lied.

"While I acknowledge that your hyper-diligence with work would definitely manifest in this type of ledger, that doesn't explain why it's screaming," he replied.

Honestly, I couldn't hear the screams.

I wonder why not?

Because I was causing them?

I wonder....

I mean, I knew *why* it was screaming. If indeed it was screaming. The problem with killing people is that then their ghosts can run around and tell on you. This was an issue that I needed to negotiate, so I trapped all of their souls in that ledger. Problem solved. Unfortunately, I didn't know they had been screaming this entire time.

"Oh, really? It's screaming?" I asked as I quickly crossed the room and took the book from him, putting it near my ear as if to listen. "I don't hear anything. Are you sure it's not just the party downstairs? It's quite loud."

That whole exercise made me feel quite stupid and silly.

"You really can't hear it? You can't hear the screams?" he asked.

I sighed and put the book back down on the side table where my brother had found it. And I stared at it.

My obsessive-compulsive nature had gotten the best of me. There are some things you just shouldn't write down. And a list of all the people you have killed is one of them. But that was the way I had managed to trap their souls in the ledger. It was really a kind of catch-22. I guess I should've used invisible ink....

"No, I can't hear anything from it," I replied as I tapped the book with my finger.

"I wish you were lying," he said.

"Why?"

"Why? Because that tells me you killed these people, didn't you? Or had them killed. Somehow," Ozzie said, his pleading eyes penetrating into my heart. Or what was left of my heart. "And their souls are screaming out for help, but you can't hear it because you're the cause."

"Hmmmmm?" was all I could manage as a reply.

"You know I can tell when you're lying, which is why you aren't saying anything. You're a terrible liar."

My eyes traveled up from the ledger and met his.

"Was this a directive from work?" he continued.

I smiled at him.

Well, there was no going back now.

He had figured almost all of it out on his own.

"I always said you were smarter than you looked," I said as I flopped down onto the plush couch next to the table and cracked my neck.

"Again, was this a directive from work???" he insisted, pointing angrily at the ledger.

"Not exactly," I replied.

"Why would you kill all of these people?!?!" he shouted at me.

"If you had done your job in the first place, I wouldn't have had to take the matter on," I answered. "I was told to kill the next Jainkohiltzaile before he or she could gain their powers. So this is the logical solution."

"What's the logical solution?"

"Kill all of the lejerdemani. That's what I've determined to be the solution."

He stared at me like I had just grown five more heads. And not in the good way.

"Have you ever stopped to think that the Jainkohiltzaile exists for a reason?" he asked.

I returned his glare with a glare of my own.

"Whatever that reason is—your *girlfriend* has been entirely useless in that regard," I threw back at him. "She does nothing. We might as well not have a Jainkohiltzaile at all. Which is apparently exactly what the gods want."

"She..." he started to say.

"*Shhheee,*" I said in the most mocking tone I

could muster. "Does nothing. She hangs around with you and Archie all day, every day, year after year. Is that the true purpose of a Jainko-hiltzaile??? She is soft. She is a coward. She has avoided her job completely, but I haven't. It's not my fault that I'm the only one who's been working and doing my proper duty."

"Your duty?! How was *this* your proper duty? Genocide couldn't have possibly been an assignment, Riot. And do you think we exist just to work? That we were created just to work?" he asked.

Tears had started to form in his eyes.

He was as soft as his soft girlfriend.

"There's no point in crying about this. What else is there besides work? I believe we are here to work, and nothing else," I answered.

"Those people. Those lejerdemani. They were not your work. They had lives and purposes and you took that away. You weren't supposed to kill all these people, Riot. How could you kill all of these people?"

"Look at yourself, Ozzie. You are a God of Death! I am a God of Death. That is what we do. We kill people. Well, I kill people while you goof off and get emotionally attached to something you shouldn't even...."

"Is that what this is *really* about? This is about Sylvie and me? You've murdered hundreds, if not thousands of people, because you think I shouldn't be with Sylvie???"

"I think you were slow and useless. And still are honestly. I think you should've gotten to her before she became the Jainkohiltzaile. And I think you should've killed her then. Actually, I *know* you should've killed her then. But you didn't. You couldn't, and here we are."

"So this is somehow all my fault?"

I rolled my eyes.

"Well—truthfully—that *is* how I see it," I said and scowled.

He picked up the ledger again.

There was little point in me keeping it away from him now.

He scanned the pages. And his tears started flowing more quickly.

"You haven't killed a single Coventry or Welser," he said.

"I was waiting until I had to."

"Then somewhere deep inside that twisted mind of yours you knew this was wrong. You didn't kill my friends."

"I will eventually. I wasn't *not* killing them because they're your friends, you stupid man."

"How can you say that? How can you do that?"

"I just haven't done it yet because they haven't yet come up as the ancestors of the Jainkohiltzaile. Also, if I start doing that Archie will probably notice, and then eventually you and Sylvie would get clued in. Although I highly doubt she'd ever actually kill me, I don't want to present her with such an obvious reason to do so by being caught killing Henry or Horace or something."

"How can you talk about this all so nonchalantly?!"

"Should I talk about this with chalance instead? I don't think that's a word—but I think I've already made my point."

"I can't even fathom your point. I have to show this to Sylvie. And Archie and everyone. You can't keep doing this," he said as he held up the ledger and shook it in the air.

"On the contrary, I can do whatever I need to do."

I held out my arm and dragged my fingernail up from my wrist past my elbow to draw a line of blood out. And yes, gods have blood in them. I know, you readers are probably shocked by this information.

And then I cast a powerful transformation spell. One taught to me by Horace. In fact, he invented this one. Is that some type of irony?

The blood was necessary to make the spell strong enough to fuse my brother with the cabinet that stood across the room from me. And to keep him in that form. No matter what spells he tried of his own.

He would look so lovely in this pleasant sitting room, and no one would ever know he was here.

"What are you doing now? Stop that," Ozzie said as he reached toward my newly wounded arm.

"*Eraldatu orain, nire anaia,*" I said as I quickly stood up, grabbed him by the throat, and stared into his eyes. "Transform now, my brother."

"What could you possibly be trying to do?" he choked out.

Those were his last words to me.

He dissolved into a black liquidy cloud that disappeared into the Boulle cabinet.

Or armoire.

Are we calling it an armoire or a cabinet?

I can't decide.

Despite being a God of Death, I couldn't actually kill my brother, as he was also a god. Only Sylvie can do that, in theory. So he would be a cabinet instead. Or an armoire. Whichever label we are going with here.

The slice on my arm burned.

"*Itxi*, close," I ordered and the wound healed, the blood vanished.

My ledger was on the floor where Ozzie had dropped it as he vaporized. I picked it up and walked over to the cabinet.

Which is where you first came in on this situation, dear reader.

Looking back I shouldn't have done that. I shouldn't have transformed Ozzie. I don't know what I should've done instead. But this set off a series of events, a domino game of lies, that ended with me being transformed myself. Which was very unfortunate.

But I'm getting ahead of myself.

I looked at the ledger. And despite my hesitance to touch the armoire, which was now also my brother, I unlocked one of the drawers, put the ledger in it, and locked it in there.

"Now you can think about that ledger for the rest of eternity," I said to him. "You'll even have to listen to the screams of their souls. Well, you'll have to do that for me because I can't hear them anyway."

"Who are you talking to?" Sylvie asked me as she walked into the room.

"Ah, just myself. Pondering if I should get a Boulle desk for my office. He made such fine pieces, didn't he?" I asked her as I swept my arm toward my brother the armoire.

She looked at me funny. But then again, she normally did that. So it wasn't anything new.

"Have you seen Ozzie around here? He said he'd meet me in this room. We were trying to hide from Henry's party downstairs. It's getting a little out of hand," she giggled slightly, but in that uncomfortable way people do during meaningless conversations.

I had to think fast.

"Oh, he was just here. He told me to let you know that he was going to go look at that Kahlo painting that Henry is going to hang in one of the music rooms. I believe it's still in one of the storage rooms though."

"Alright, I'll go look for him," she said as she

turned and walked out of the room.

I had bought myself some time.

But looking for Ozzie in a storage room was going to be a wild goose chase. Sure, there were a lot of storage rooms, but not enough to keep her endlessly engaged. So I'd have to piece together a plan to get rid of her as quickly as possible. And it would have to involve trickery. The instant she suspected me of wrongdoing—my life would be in danger.

Where was Tiziano when I needed him most?

He was always so good at skullduggery.

Fast-forward to a few hours later when I'm standing next to Sylvie in a storage room, armed with a plan. I had led her to the Kahlo painting— yes, dear reader—it did exist.

But of course Ozzie was nowhere to be found.

"I think this is the Kahlo," I said. "Even though it doesn't look like her."

"Oh, it's not a self-portrait. It's Lupe Marín, the volatile second wife of Diego Rivera. And she's the one who sliced and diced the painting up after having an argument with Frida," Sylvie explained.

"Wait, I thought Kahlo was married to Rivera?"

"Oh she was—but she was his third wife, after Lupe. And then later his fourth wife, after herself," she said, smiling. "It's complicated."

"Well, men, right? Men. But anyway, should we go inside and see if Ozzie is in there? He must've gone inside it. He's always wanted to meet Kahlo."

"Might as well," she replied, shrugging. "I've been looking in storage rooms all over the place for hours, and he's just nowhere to be found."

My plan was working.

As we went inside the painting, I smiled—knowing that there was really no reason my plan could fail. Because Sylvie didn't realize she shouldn't trust me.

Was she just stupid or naïve? I'm not sure.

Ozzie had shielded her from reality for far too long. Gods should just not be trusted. Everyone knew that. Well, everyone with a clue.

"Where's Ozzie? And where's Lupe?" Sylvie asked upon our arrival.

Luckily Lupe's chair was empty, so I didn't have to deal with that issue.

"I feel funny," Sylvie said as she quickly sat down on the floor of Frida's painting studio.

"Ozzie isn't here. Lupe's probably off yelling at

Rivera and Kahlo somewhere, and you feel funny because this painting was just coated with an experimental poison before we went into it," I answered.

"An experimental what?"

"An experimental poison that drains any lejerdemani of their strength and energy when it's applied to them, through one method or another. Amazingly, it seems to work even when used in this manner."

"Why? Why aren't you sick?"

"I'm a god. Not a lejerdemani. It doesn't apply to me."

"Who would put that on the painting? How do you know about it?"

"I put it there—to poison you."

Her breathing slowed significantly as she continued to stare at me.

The faint light of realization slowly crept across her face.

"Are you trying to kill me?"

"Well, you know I can't do that. I wish I could. But I lack the ability. For now, I've poisoned you, disarming your ability to kill me, and then I'll leave you here in this painting."

"Where's Ozzie? What did you do to him?"

"Hmmm. I see the loving girlfriend is more concerned about the welfare of her lover than herself."

"What did you do to him?" she asked again.

"Do you think he'll even remember you?"

She returned my stare but didn't reply.

"Let's talk about humans," I said, buying Tiziano and Ischia enough time to get set up in the storage room to execute the second part of this plan. "Well, humans toil away day after day, right? 24 hours a day. 365 days a year. Year after year. Or whatever stupid measurement of time it is that they've created.

"But for all those days spent living they maybe remember one big thing that happened each year. So-and-so got married. That's the year we went on vacation to that place. I started college that year. We had a baby. Etc. Etc. So on and so forth. All that time spent breathing and working and sweating, all that mundane day-to-day junk, boils down to perhaps one memory for every year. All that living—for nothing. And all that living *is* for nothing.

"And for gods, well, it's even worse. Nothing ever happens to us. No weddings or funerals or vacations or surgeries or all those things that stick into human brains as memories. None of that. Nothing. So do you think he'll even remember you? You're just a blip. Just that little speck of dust that gets in your eye for an instant and then it's gone. You're blinked away. Do you think your existence means anything in the life of an immortal?"

"It doesn't matter what I say to you now," Sylvie said. "You've clearly already made your mind up about me. You aren't going to tell me where Ozzie is. That's also clear. Or tell me what you've done to him."

Sylvie tried to move her arms, but she could barely even twitch a shoulder. The poison had been quite successful. Thank you again, Horace.

"Ozzie's gone, my dear. He's left you."

"That's not possible."

"Why not? He and I finally agreed that the Jainkohiltzaile needed to be eliminated. His original objective will now be complete."

"What do you mean? Ozzie isn't like that."

"Ah, the dim brain of the lejerdemani," I said, smiling at her. "I want you to remember this was your second chance to kill a god, but you failed yet again. I was smarter and faster than you. I've been killing off lejerdemani left and right—hunting down the next Jainkohiltzaile, and you haven't even noticed. You blind imbecile. I've always watched you so closely to see the gears turning in your tiny head. But nothing's ever actually happening up there. No thoughts. No epiphanies. No sudden brilliance. And that's why you'll rot in this painting until you're dead. I hope I never see you again, Sylvie."

And with that I snapped my fingers and left the painting.

"Now! Faster!" I screamed at Tiziano and Ischia as they threw cursed paint onto the canvas that I had just emerged from.

The poison had worked on Sylvie, despite her being the Jainkohiltzaile. But it hadn't killed her, and I had no idea how long it would be effective on her. She could follow me out at any moment, so the canvas had to be thoroughly coated as quickly as possible.

If you're wondering where I came up with the idea of cursed paint to cover up a canvas and trap someone inside a painting—well, you guessed it —Horace Welser.

Of course, that concept didn't really come from a conversation on how to trap someone inside a painting. It was more a discussion of how to seal a magical painting. Tomato, tomaatoh though. As long as it kept Sylvie out of my hair.

Soon the canvas was covered with so much cursed paint that surely the image we had gone into—the world I had left Sylvie in—was no longer escapable.

Ugh, she was such a stupid child. But now she would be stuck in there until her time as the Jainkohiltzaile was up. She would slowly lose all of her powers, and she would die.

Tiziano, Ischia, and I stood staring at the painting, each of us panting and exhausted.

"Hey guys, have you seen Ozzie?" Archie asked as he walked into the storage room.

(A Note to Our Dear Marvelous Author from Riot: If people could stop walking in on me just as I am finishing a heinous deed, that would be great. Thank you.

Dear Riot, from The Marvelous Author: Have you ever blown your nose and then hours later discovered a dried up piece of snot on your nose? And then you're like—*damn*, that's been hanging off the side of my nose for hours! How gross must it have looked? How many people saw that? Ew. I'm hideous.

No? That's never happened to you before?

It was just me? Well then, never mind. Cough.

<u>Another Note to Our Dear Marvelous Author from Riot</u>: I don't even know why I bother trying to talk to you.

<u>Dear Riot, from The Marvelous Author</u>: Honestly, I don't know why anyone even tries to have a sane conversation with me. Back to the story....)

Ischia's eyes widened as she looked at me in panic. Tiziano looked like he wanted to lunge forward and knock Archie unconscious, so he wouldn't remember what he just walked in on.

"Uh, whatcha guys doin' in here?" Archie continued with a clearly perplexed look on his face.

"The Goddess of History," I began to invent a lie. "What was her name again? Tori something? She was just here."

"*What?!* Why? Gosh, I hate her," Archie said as he got slightly flustered.

Archie and Tori had a long-standing feud. And she was the only person I had ever seen actually irritate him. Facts I would use to my advantage in this situation.

"She stole a painting!" I half-yelled, acting

shocked. "And Ozzie and Sylvie had just gone inside of it! The Frida Kahlo that Henry was going to hang soon. Tori showed up and took it. We tried to stop her, but she just threw this cursed paint at us. We just barely managed to get out of the way! It all went on this other painting behind us! And then she left."

"Gone!" Tiziano added, unnecessarily.

"Poof. She disappeared!" Ischia punctuated the lie, also unnecessarily.

"*What the?!?!*" Archie asked, preparing to swear.

"She said it should be in her collection, and not yours," I continued.

"It all happened so fast," Ischia said as she nodded.

"Tiziano will go with you to find the painting, Archie," I said. "He'll help you track it down and find Sylvie and Ozzie."

"Well, I'm sure those two will just leave the painting eventually, and tell me where it ended up," Archie said, scratching his chin.

"Look at this cursed paint though! Who knows what she intends on doing with the painting. You know, she's got all those silly little hiding places throughout time for her collection, but they are all sealed in stupid ways. What if that magic blocks Sylvie and Ozzie from coming back out of the painting?!" I exclaimed.

God, that was mentally painful. But I hoped my very, very poor acting ability would help me in this situation. It was only Ozzie who could tell when I was lying. Archie had never paid that much attention to me to notice such things.

"Dammit, you're right. She does have all those 'Treasure Chests of Time,' as she calls them," Archie replied. "Who knows what kind of seal those things have. And I've never seen that kind of cursed paint before. I wonder where she got it from? If she can do that—well, you know she always teases me about taking back what is rightfully hers. But the painting is destroyed, right? Destroyed. And this is The Realm of Destruction. Why is this such a difficult concept for her?"

"Well, you better get moving," I interrupted him. "The faster you follow her the easier it'll be to find the painting, right? Ischia will stay here to see if Sylvie and Ozzie make it back on their own. And I'll ask Henry and Horace if they can help us."

"Alright. Tiziano, let's start visiting the places where Tori might have taken the painting.

'Treasure Chests of Time,' more like 'Treasure Chests of Crime'!" Archie said.

He always enjoyed rhyming just a little more than a normal person should enjoy rhyming.

I lifted my chin toward Tiziano as they left the room, cocked my head to the left, and narrowed my gaze, sending my faithful minion the facial expression that meant: 'Occupy him as long as possible.'

Several minutes later, after we had stood very still to catch our breath and recover our sense of composure, Ischia eventually commented: "I hope he has a good idea for how to keep Archie occupied."

"Oh, Tiziano's full of excellent ideas. I'm sure he'll come up with something. But clearly we need to figure out a way to kill a god ourselves," I replied.

"What?"

"Kill Archie. Somehow we have to figure out a way to do that."

"Why would we do that?"

"To make sure he doesn't interfere with our plans."

"But he's mine."

"*Is he?* I'm pretty sure he's asexual given the

fact that he's never appeared to be interested in anyone."

"Well, even if he is, he's still mine."

"So we should keep him around and let him destroy all of our hard work?"

"I...."

"Speaking of ideas, you come up with something to prevent Your Lover-Boy from blowing the whistle on us to the lejerdemani. Particularly Horace, since we need his help as much as possible, even if he doesn't know it. If you can't come up with a better plan though, we have to kill Archie."

"But how will you kill a god if you aren't the Jainkohiltzaile?"

"Good question. And an excellent one to bring up with Horace, in a round-about way, of course."

Ischia usually agreed with everything that came out of my mouth. That was sort of her raison d'être. Sure, she could be playful and silly. But this wasn't her being playful. This was her wanting to keep Archie for herself.

But what were we going to tell him? What could we possibly say that would make him take our side in this situation and not Horace and

Henry's side? Because they would most likely *not* agree with my plan to kill all of the lejerdemani—since they were themselves lejerdemani. Hmmmmm.

"You ladies are going to miss it!" Horace said as he walked into the storage room and waved at us to follow him.

How do all these people keep finding us??? This house is literally ten city blocks of Fifth Avenue mansions combined! Usually people get lost every five minutes in this place.

"Miss what???" Ischia asked him as she led him back out of the room. Hopefully quickly enough that he didn't notice the Kahlo covered in cursed paint.

I snapped my fingers and sent that item to my office in the Realm of the Dead until I could come up with a plan on how to more efficiently hide it.

"Henry and I have a big announcement! And Archie too! Where's Archie? Have you seen him?" Horace asked.

I trailed behind, following them to the heart of Henry's 'The House of Coventry Annual Halloween Bash,' full of annoying people.

Ischia lied endlessly to Horace about not having seen Archie at all, nor Sylvie. Nor Ozzie.

Well, she hadn't exactly seen Ozzie or Sylvie. So I guess those weren't lies.

We entered the main hall, a cavernous space fit for royalty and state balls, where Henry stood up on a balcony looking down on all of us. Horace scurried up the stairs to join him. He shrugged as he informed him that Archie was MIA.

"Ladies and gentlemen, boys and girls!" Henry bellowed out to all of the twittering, twit-faced guests. "I wanted all three of us to make this announcement today—Horace, Archie, and I. But our dear God of Destruction is off frolicking somewhere in the dark corners of this wonderful party, haha.

"I'd wait until he shows up, eventually, to make this announcement but the cake is supposed to come out soon. And I don't want to hold up that delightful activity, or Jennifer will roast me royally if I mess up her pastry delivery schedule!"

Everyone giggled in reply.

God, I hate this stuff.

I looked over at Jennifer, the house chef and a plump purple dragon, as she scowled from a doorway up at Henry. Behind her was a massive stacked-jack-o-lantern-themed cake, probably about seven feet tall, on a cart, waiting to be rolled out into the hall to the oooo's and aaaa's of the guests.

She tapped her clawed foot in frustration on the marble floor. The fact that the cake was meant to be served a half an hour ago was written all over her craggy, scaled face.

I had always appreciated her work ethic, but I never understood why she put up with such an airhead as a boss. Henry did nothing but grate on my already-raw nerves, not to mention the fact that what he was about to say was going to make me into his full-blown enemy.

"Five years ago, Horace, Archie, and myself created a new kind of being. We called him a Lastang. But then we gave him a real name, of course. Tom, come up here," Henry said, waving down to a man in the audience.

As Tom emerged from the crowd, I tried not to let my discomfort show on my face. He had an aura of power I had never seen before in my life. All around him was a swirling cloud of vibrating red lines.

"Do you see those?" I whispered to Ischia.

"See what? Tom? I guess that's Tom," she said

as she shrugged and gestured toward him.

"No, do you see his aura, those red squiggles all around him?"

"I don't see anything like that. I see that he's wearing sunglasses though. Inside. During a party. At night. That's weird, right?"

"He's not the only idiot at this party wearing sunglasses," I answered.

In fact, about a third of the people in the room had them on.

But more importantly, was I the only one who could see the red lines?

No one else in the crowd seemed to be discussing them or pointing them out.

They made me quite uncomfortable. Somehow, despite them not having eyes, I felt like the lines were looking at me, watching me. Meeting my gaze.

"Creating and training Tom, well, really crafting him—has taken those five long years. But we think we have perfected him and he's ready for his purpose!" Henry announced, and then clapped.

The audience applauded as well.

Morons.

They didn't even know what they were applauding.

"What do you think he is?" Ischia asked me under her breath.

"I have no idea. But whatever it is, I don't like it."

"Tom is the first-ever hand-crafted demi-god. Built with the sole purpose of hunting down and eliminating whatever has been causing all of these deaths amongst the lejerdemani," Henry said as Tom reached the top of the stairs and turned to face all of us partygoers.

This time the crowd erupted. Clapping. Yelling. Screams. Gasps. Foot-stomping. More clapping. Confetti being thrown in the air.

Ischia grabbed my hand in reflex. I quickly flicked it off of mine.

"Don't be obvious," I said.

"*What is he?!?*" she whispered.

"A problem," I answered.

"Tom is the first," Horace continued. "But recently we have crafted twelve more Lastangs and soon they will start patrolling all of the Realms looking for the reason our lives have been shadowed by so much grief."

And out marched twelve more of them from the hallways behind the balcony.

"*Ayyye*, a big, big problem," I whispered.

"What are we going to do now?" Ischia whimpered.

"I'm still a god," I said to her quietly. "And they are only demi-gods. Even if Horace makes a thousand, I'll still figure out a way to defeat them. Now applaud and smile like your life depends on it. Let's pretend this is the best news of our life."

Ischia screamed with faux glee and fist pumped the air, jumping up and down like the hyper poodle she was. I mean, she isn't actually a dog. She has just always reminded me of a poodle. I smiled and clapped like a politician's not-so-secretly exasperated wife.

I felt an overwhelming urge to write down all of the lies I had told that day. To keep track of them, of course, and to tally up all of the problems I had to solve. I had a lot of those. But then I remembered my ledger, and how some things just shouldn't be written down.

(Dear Riot, from The Marvelous Author: Today a piece of shredded wheat fell into my coffee, and I retrieved it. But in the act of retrieving it I managed to drop it back into the coffee, and instead of floating on the surface like it was before—it sunk down into the darkness never to be seen again.

Or to be seen again when I finished the cup of coffee. Then I would find it sitting at the bottom of the cup. So I said to myself: the heck with it. So now I'm drinking the world's first cup of shredded wheat coffee. I'm such an amazing innovator.

A Note to Our Dear Marvelous Author from Riot: I don't know why I even tried to write a cool ending to this chapter when you came along and messed it up with this stupid junk. Sigh.)

ANOTHER INTERRUPTION.

By Maple, the Magnificent Author of this Amazing Story.

(Maple: Okay, what should we read about next?

Penny: You haven't said a single thing yet about Verbena. When are we going to learn about that part of the story?

Maple: Well, I didn't want to get into that yet.

Penny: Why not?

Maple: Because it'll probably make you pretty angry with me.

Penny: I'm *already* angry with you.

Maple: Oh.)

CHAPTER FIVE.

Naomi's Thoughts.

Beginning at that Same Halloween Party.

By Naomi.

(Maple: Okay, Naomi you have to write this next part.

Naomi: What? Who you are? Who let you in here?

Maple: I'm the author of this incredible book. Duh.

Naomi: And I am?

Maple: One of my amazing characters, and the mother of Ellie, Nora, and Morrow Demington.

Naomi: I don't remember having any children. Wait, I'm only 15 years old!!

Maple: Well, you're only 15 right now in this moment when I'm harassing you to write my book for me. You age, like a bitter wine.

Naomi: Oh. But wait, who's this Demington person I marry???

Maple: Well, here's the thing—you have to continue telling the story to find out.

Naomi: That sucks.

Maple: I think you meant to say, 'That's a wonderful idea. Let me do that right now!'

Naomi: No, I meant to say, 'That sucks.')

As I watched my grandfather wave to the ecstatic crowd from his balcony, I thought about how embarrassed I was.

Yes, yes. I should've been beaming with pride and screaming alongside everyone else who was now patting me on the back and grinning at me. As if by just being his granddaughter I had somehow contributed to this miracle.

And that was the problem. This would have to be a miracle.

My grandfather and Horace had basically just announced that they had solved the biggest crisis the lejerdemani have ever faced. It was a tall order to say that they had cracked the case before they had even started pursuing the criminal, or criminals.

Perhaps there was more to it all than I knew or understood. But as I shifted my gaze to this Tom fellow's completely expressionless face, I wondered if what was going on in his brain, somewhere behind those stupid sunglasses, was enough to save us.

Who knew that this Halloween party would mark the day when my life changed forever.

No really. *Who knew that stuff?* Someone should've told me ahead of time so I could've mentally prepared myself.

The morning after the party I found myself sitting across the breakfast table from Tom, who seemed to be staring at me intently with that completely expressionless face from behind those stupid sunglasses.

He didn't move.

He didn't blink.

I was pretty sure he wasn't even breathing.

In the kitchen my best friend Penny and my sister Verbena were cooking up breakfast.

I wasn't allowed in kitchens anymore after 'The Hot Dog Incident.' Which is when my shadow creature, a miniature Galloway calf named Lemmie (short for Lemur), found me in the kitchen cooking beef hot dogs for lunch. He was so upset that he blew up the oven, nearly killing me, and then he cursed me forever so that whenever I even start to cook something—the oven explodes.

So I'm not allowed in kitchens anymore.

I have asked Lemmie several times for a removal of said curse. But he always says that if my powers were strong enough, I could remove it myself. I think that's his backbuttwards way of encouraging me.

Speaking of Lemmie, he was sitting next to me at the table, also staring at the non-breathing Tom.

Last night had turned into a panic-fest on the part of my grandfather and Horace, Penny's grandfather. Archie went missing and was never found. And he was the god of our Realm. So he was kinda an important person.

Ozzie and Sylvie had also gone missing. Riot and Ischia couldn't find them and went off to look for them. Tiziano had already been looking for Archie when the Lastang announcement was made.

Then my grandfather declared that this distressing and bizarre situation necessitated an immediate change in living arrangements. Verbena and I were sent to live with Penny's family in Pipistrelle Village in the Earthly Realm.

Our parents also joined us. But it seemed as if both Penny's parents and our parents were going to be spending a lot of time with the twelve other Lastangs, trying to find a way to counter whatever was killing us all off.

Which is why it was further decided, without any input from Verbena or myself, that my sister and I would join Penny at the normal human high school.

Penny had gone to human school since she was five years old because her mother was a now-retired kindergarten teacher. God knows why anybody would ever want to be a kindergarten teacher. My impression of school, via Penny's stories, was that it was a very, very boring place.

Our parents assured us that this experience would expand our education and socialization. But I knew it was just the simplest way to keep us girls out of their hair. It was difficult to argue with them though when they're out there trying to save our species from extinction.

"What I don't get is why Tom is here. Shouldn't he be off with the others?" I asked.

"I don't get that either," Lemmie replied. "He seems pretty useless to me, just sitting here at the table."

"We're 'just sitting' at the table, too, Lemmie," I said.

"I'm not just sitting here. I'm working up a lot of stinky gas in my bowels for release later when you are eating," he replied.

"Um, well. Besides that topic, back to Tom," I said. "Maybe we're safer here on Earth with the humans than in the Realm of Destruction, where clearly all the Coventrys would be sitting ducks without Archie around. But isn't Tom supposed to be out there hunting down whatever needs hunted down?"

"Horace said he's here to guard us. So he'll pretty much be completely aware of everything we're doing at all times," Verbena explained, grimacing, as she poured pancake batter onto the griddle.

"Awkward," Penny said out of the corner of her mouth.

"I don't understand why you guys need this dude as a bodyguard. I mean, I'm right here," Eagle said as he punched his own tiny bunny chest.

"That hurt, didn't it?" Grizz, Verbena's jerboa shadow creature, asked him sarcastically as he jumped across the kitchen counter to mock Eagle more closely, aka: kick him in the chest.

Eagle went flying across the kitchen, and soon we all witnessed a swirling tornado of two rodents trying to fight each other while not actually getting injured themselves. Which basically looked like two rodents playing a really aggressive, angry game of patty-cake.

"You guys are clearly more useless than this guy as far as being bodyguards. You can't even manage to kill each other, for once," Lemmie grumbled, and then he directed his attention back to Tom. "Well, you tell us, *stud*—are you tough? Are you tough enough to protect all of us? Like battle-hardened? Like steel?"

"Horace has told me that I have a heat that stings, if that helps," Tom answered.

"Oh, I bet you do," Penny said in between giggles.

"What the *heck* does that even mean?" Eagle asked, as he choked on a hash brown while trying to talk and eat at the same time.

"I am not sure," Tom replied.

"And is your name *really* Tom?" Grizz asked

him.

The jerboa then hopped up onto the table and stood directly on top of Tom's stack of pancakes, which he'd been about to eat. Grizz glared at the interloper up close.

"No, my name isn't really Tom. But that's what Horace told me to go by. So it will work fine in this situation."

He then started to eat the pancakes, despite the fact that there was a rodent on top of them.

"Uh-huh," Grizz said.

He continued to stare at Tom for a little while. Then he hopped to the other side of the table and sat down on the corner farthest away from Tom.

"And do you really need to eat food? Or can you just survive on the blood of your enemies?" Grizz continued, still attempting to stare Tom down, which is sort of difficult to do when your opponent is wearing sunglasses.

"I do need to eat. Although I often survive on the blood of magical rodents that talk too much," Tom replied and then he stuffed three whole pancakes into his mouth at once.

"Harumph," Grizz grunted. "Very funny. But I'll have you know that I was hunting down and capturing criminals before you were even invented!"

"You hunted down criminals, Grizz?" I asked him, genuinely surprised.

"No, not really. It just sounded cool to say that."

"So wait, if you were invented five years ago, how old does that make you?" Verbena asked Tom.

"You do look around our age, sort of," Penny added with a sly grin on her face.

"I am not very old."

"*What the heck does that even mean?*" Eagle scoffed. It was becoming his catch phrase.

"I will be sixteen according to the paperwork forged to get me into the high school that you three girls are attending," Tom replied.

"Wait, you're going to go to school with us, too?!?!" I asked, my stomach dropping.

I hadn't really been too enthusiastic about this high school idea. Well, that's an understatement. I had hated it completely from the instant I was told about it, and had been dreading it from my head to my toes.

"I will be with the three of you at all times."

"Doesn't that mean that the three of us then have to be together at all times?" Verbena asked.

"Well, you have to at least be in the same building as me for efficiency purposes. If you are in the same vicinity, I will be able to listen to what you are doing," Tom said and nodded.

"Listen?" I gulped.

"My hearing ability allows me to listen in on anything happening within a one mile radius of my body."

"Like, you'll even be able to hear what we do in the bathroom?!?" Penny gasped.

"Yes, I heard everything you did in the bathroom earlier this morning, for example."

Penny's face lost its coloring, completely.

"Man," she whined. "I was going to ask you to pretend to be my boyfriend once we started going to school tomorrow! So everyone there finally realizes that I'm not a total loser. But now I'm just too mortified to look you in the eye!"

She held her head in her hands as she leaned on the kitchen counter.

"Good thing he never takes off those sunglasses then. You'll never have the opportunity to look him in the eye anyways," Eagle said and laughed.

"Speaking of boyfriends—you know, Tom, my little Naomi is available," Lemmie said, and pointed to me, while smirking. "She doesn't have a boyfriend. In fact, she's never had one. Ever. Like a royal loser."

"I know Naomi doesn't have a boyfriend," Tom said.

Oh. Great. Why does he even need to know that?!?

"That's totally irrelevant!" I yelped.

"I have received complete dossiers on all six of you," Tom added as he finished the last pancake on the table and followed that up with the last sausage. "Whether or not anyone has a boyfriend is actually relevant, as one of them may be trying to murder lejerdemani and they would have to be investigated thoroughly."

"Oh, well it's a good thing that all these ladies are sad singles then," Eagle snickered. "Totally single."

"I'd kill you, if I could," Penny told him.

"Wait, you've eaten all the food, Tom," Verbena said as she came over to sit down at the table. To eat. Food that was no longer there.

"Yes, yes I did."

"But none of us had eaten yet," she said, motioning to our completely empty plates and bowls.

"No, no you hadn't."

"Some of that was for us, you numbskull!" Penny cried out.

"Ah, I see. I will make more for you then," Tom said as he got up and went into the kitchen to make breakfast. Again.

He tied on an apron featuring kittens dancing while holding oversized-spoons. It was quite the finishing touch on his outfit, which was a black t-shirt, black jeans, and black Converse.

"That was more than enough food for ten people," Penny groaned. "I can't believe you ate all that by yourself!"

"*Prandium cibum*, breakfast food," Verbena said, casting a spell to fill the fridge back up with groceries.

"Someday we'll have the ability to make all of this food again just by snapping our fingers," Penny said and sighed.

"But today is not that day," Eagle said, grinning.

"You know, you shadow creatures could do that for us," Verbena said. "You could make breakfast again in an instant."

"But where's the fun in that? I like seeing you toil," Grizz said as he laid down on the table, and propped his head up in his tiny paws to stare at Verbena with mocking affection.

"Do not worry. I can manage this," Tom announced as he opened the fridge.

Quickly casting one spell after another he managed to re-create all of the breakfast dishes Penny and Verbena had made, plus about ten more, within a matter of ten seconds. To say that my sister, Penny, and I were slack-jawed at this display of skill would've been an understatement.

"And he did it all while wearing an apron with kittens on it," Penny whispered as she gazed lovingly at the food, and then at Tom.

"You guys are too easily impressed," Eagle said.

"I *am* impressed and that confirms it," Verbena said and smiled at me. "Naomi, you're just gonna have to marry Tom. Because you can't cook, and clearly he's a professional!"

"Hey, we haven't tasted it yet though," Lemmie grunted. "It could taste like rat doodoo."

"Here, Lemmie, have a beef sausage," Penny said, grinning at him while offering him the newly-piled-high plate.

"There's a special place in Hell for you, Penny Welser," he replied.

"Guys, Tom's a bodyguard. Not a chef," I interjected, still thinking about how Verbena just told me I should marry him when he was looking toward me.

My face was on fire.

"That's right, that's right," Penny said. "So you'll marry him for his body, too! Get it? Bodyguard? Body? Because he's got such a hot body? Get it?"

"You know, your jokes become less jokey when you explain them like that," Eagle said, poking Penny in the ribs after he jumped up next to her at the table.

"Does that qualify as sexual harassment in the workplace, Tom?" Grizz asked him.

"Does what qualify?" Tom asked, as he rejoined us at the table.

"Were you even paying attention?" Lemmie asked.

"I pay attention to everything."

"What's the problem guys? C'mon," Penny continued. "He's totally hot. Look at him. He's so hot I'm practically singed by the heat over here. Six foot four-ish and buff. Naomi should date him. Wait, I should date him. Why am I giving him to you? I mean, he's going to be around us

24-7. It's like a built-in boyfriend!"

"Penny, would you stop obsessing about this boyfriend issue," I said and sighed.

"Would you prefer to talk about your brand-new life in human high school instead?" she asked, her voice dripping with sarcasm.

"No. Absolutely not."

"Okay, new topic. Not about high school. Those are off-limit words," Verbena said as she whimpered a little bit, just slightly. "Instead, Tom, why do you wear sunglasses all the time?"

"Verbena! You can't just ask a freak why he wears freakish sunglasses all the freakish time!" Grizz mocked.

"They are protection," Tom replied.

"Protection from what?" Penny asked.

"They protect those around me."

"Wait, they protect us from you?" I asked.

"Yes, that's right," he said.

Verbena, Penny, and I exchanged worried looks.

"Can you explain how? In simple sentences?" Penny asked.

"My eyes are designed to read guilt. When I take off these special glasses, which block the power of my eyes, everyone around me is then flooded with feelings of guilt for every wrong they've ever committed in their life."

"Oh god, Eagle. You'd probably stroke out given the amount of heinous crap you've put me through these past few years," Penny said.

"Then as people feel that guilt, I process it," Tom finished.

"So you're saying that your eyes aren't just sensitive to light?" Eagle teased him.

"Um, no. It's more that you are all sensitive to my eyes."

"Do it," Grizz prodded him. "Take off your glasses, let's see what happens!"

"Do it. Do it. Do it," Eagle said, clapping in time with his own chanting.

"There is little point. I am pretty sure that three teenage girls have not been murdering thousands of lejerdemani before they were even born."

"Good point. Good point," Grizz replied.

"But this way we can feel how it works, and you can test your skills on us," Lemmie nodded. "It'll be educational."

"I hope you realize that it's only our shadow creatures who are asking you to take off your glasses," Verbena added. "The rest of us *sane* individuals have no interest in re-living the guilt of lying to our parents about having candy hidden in our bedroom or something."

"Is *that* the worst thing you've done in your life Verbena? Pssshhhh," Eagle said and laughed.

"C'mon Tom, just lower your glasses slightly. I'm a bit of a masochist. I'd love to re-live the guilt of my past," Grizz explained as he hopped toward Tom and tried to jump up and grab his sunglasses.

"He's not a circus sideshow," I said.

"How about I just look at you, Grizz?" Tom asked and smiled.

"Oh my poop, that's menacing," Grizz replied. "First time I've seen this boy smile and that was damn creepy. No thanks. No thanks. I've changed my mind! And don't ever smile again. That was horrific."

"Wait. I just realized something. Do your eyes work on *normal humans*???" Penny inquired.

"Yes."

"So you're going to have to wear those things at school?!?!" she asked.

"Yes, I will have to wear them at school. I have been identified as having an 'eyesight issue' and the glasses are necessary for my health."

"*Oh. My. God,*" Penny said as she knocked her forehead on the table.

"Okay, that's it. I'm too curious. Just show us your freaky magical power guilt eyeballs," Eagle said as he stood up on the table in front of Tom. "Grizz may be too much of a chicken to look at them. But I'm not."

And in an instant Eagle snatched off his glasses while spinning around in the air.

Which was really an unnecessarily dramatic act.

"His eyeballs! They're solid black! Solid black!" Eagle exclaimed as he rudely pointed at Tom's eyes and danced on the tabletop like a loon. "That's gonna give me nightmares, man!"

"I would have just taken them off if you really wanted me to," Tom said quietly as the six of us were instantly physically overwhelmed by a flood of emotions.

Penny started sobbing with her head on the table. Verbena stood up and began pacing the room with her arms crossed. Lemmie, Eagle, and Grizz fell into fits of laughter.

And I just sat there paralyzed, thinking about all the things I had ever said and done that had hurt people. I felt my throat close up, and my eyes begin to water. Tom took his sunglasses from Eagle and put them back on.

Black.

Eyeballs.

Black.

Freaking.

Eyeballs.

That was all that was going through my head once the guilt-fest had ceased.

"And that is why I do not take my glasses off," Tom said.

"Oh my sssssss. I ddhhhh. Hoowwww? Crud," Penny stuttered, not managing to say anything with reason attached to it.

"Well, now I understand why you guys didn't just take off your glasses last night and read everyone's guilt at a party full of over a thousand people, creatures, ghosts, and gods. That would've caused pandemonium," Verbena said as she sat back down at the table, wiping tears away from the corners of her eyes.

I had started gripping the edge of the table, but was slowly loosening my hold on it. I looked over at Lemmie, who I believe had peed himself a little bit with glee.

"Man, that was *fantastic*!!!" he remarked, while

happily slapping me on the back with a hoof.

"Shadow creatures certainly experience guilt in a different way than lejerdemani do," Tom said.

"Let's do that again!" Lemmie shouted.

"Let's never, *ever* do that again," I said.

The next day at school we were going to be introduced as new transfer students. I had pretty much felt like throwing up since about four that morning. I was just slightly nervous.

Despite my sister Verbena being two years older than me, we were all put into Penny's homeroom and classes together through slightly-magically-manipulated negotiations between our parents and the school administration.

Our new homeroom teacher, Mr. Kirlby, smiled at us as we walked into the room. My sister and I followed closely behind Penny like shy lemmings. Tom stood in the doorway looking like a too-cool, almost menacing, fashion model that had accidentally walked into a high school while looking for a whitewashed wall to lean against.

"Ah, everyone—these are our new transfer students: Verbena and Naomi Coventry, and Tom Demington," Mr. Kirlby read our names from a memo.

"Wait, what?" I asked. "Did you say Demington??? His last name's *Demington*?!?!"

Penny took my hand and whispered into my ear through clenched teeth: "You're supposed to already know what his name is, you idiot. You supposedly transferred together from the same school according to the paperwork."

I blinked repeatedly in disbelief as my mouth hung open.

I stared at Tom, who smiled awkwardly at me in response.

"I marry a man with black eyeballs though, Penny," I whispered back to her.

She looked at me with complete confusion and a healthy amount of worry.

I admit that it was an appropriate response.

"Do you think he's blind?" I heard a girl whisper to her friend a few desks away from the front of the classroom.

"He doesn't have a cane or a dog though," her friend whispered back.

"Then why does he have sunglasses on?" the first girl asked.

"Aaaargghhhh," I quietly groaned.

"I don't think he's a teenager," another girl whispered. "He's like a man."

"Or a god," someone else replied. "All pouty and gorgeous."

"If he's in this school now, no girl is ever going to talk to any guy but him," a boy murmured.

"I think *I* love him, and I'm not even gay," another kid muttered.

"Which one of those girls do you think he's dating?" a girl in the back asked her friend.

This caused Penny to grin maniacally, wink at me, and violently pinch my arm with excitement.

And that marked the incredibly awkward beginning of our incredibly awkward 'normal human' high school life.

CHAPTER SIX.

*After the Party Was Over For Me,
aka: When Life Doesn't Work Out
the Way You Wanted It To.*

By Sylvie.

(Maple: Okay, Sylvie. Back to you. Tell us about
your pathetic life inside the painting after that
Halloween party.

Sylvie: Um. This story doesn't really do me
any favors, does it?

Maple: Nope.

Penny: What about Verbena?

Maple: We'll get back to her later.

Penny: You are so frustrating.

Maple: Frustrating is my middle name.)

"Ozzie's gone, my dear. He's left you."

Riot's words echoed in my ears as I lay on the
floor like a discarded rag doll.

"He and I finally agreed that the Jainkohilt-zaile needed to be eliminated. His original objective will now be complete."

How much of this had been the truth? Had Ozzie really left me? Was he now my enemy? If he was no longer mine, was there even a point to any of this? To anything? I tried to roll over, but I couldn't. I started to cry.

"I guess life is meant to be broken," I said out loud, pathetically, to myself. As the room was quite empty.

Tears rolled down my face.

Life. A glass windshield in an anchored steel frame, set against the wind. And a thousand tiny rocks keep getting slung at it. And with every new pain from the newest pebble, you wish your transparent glass would just transform into a massive boulder and fight back against the gravel of existence.

But life will always be glass. And glass can always be chipped, cracked, even broken. And there will always be some rocks that are bigger than others.

For this latest rock, hurled at me from out of nowhere, it was the unknown that was particularly puncturing for my windshield of life.

Had Ozzie really just left me here to die? And on purpose? Did I so seriously misjudge his affection for me? Well, it's not like you can force someone to love you. But that's what I thought he felt for me.

"Well, this should do it," I said as my eyes rolled from the unpleasant thoughts barreling down on me.

When I had left Old Kunkerpot's Realm to spend my days with Ozzie, instead of going around killing gods, the Four Dogs of the Apocalypse had not joined me.

I can't say that I was instantly in love with Ozzie, but I knew that I wanted to be with him. And I knew that I didn't want to live out the rest of my days sitting at my kitchen table. Staring at books. Studying. Studying. Studying.

"What about being the Jainkohiltzaile?" Muddiford had asked me. "You can't just ignore your responsibilities."

"I'll take care of that when I need to," I lied, shrugging.

I hadn't meant to lie.

It was just easier to avoid my responsibilities than face them head on.

"We'll be here when you decide you need us,"

Cadby replied, returning my shrug with one of his own.

"What do you mean? I always need you guys."

"We exist to help you be the Jainkohiltzaile," Wooferton said. "If you're not acting as the God-killer, we have no obligation to stand by your side."

"That's a bit harsh," I said.

"Yeah guys, that's a bit harsh," Beamish repeated.

"Oh. You," Wooferton said as he glared at him. "I'll deal with you soon enough, you imbecile. This is all your fault for letting in that baboonish God of Death she now wants to be with!"

"Just because I'm not out there constantly murdering gods doesn't mean you guys can't be with me."

"That's exactly what it means," Wooferton replied. "And it's not a constant job. You have to kill one about every 50 years or so. And it's not murder. It's justice."

"Also, do you think we're all imbeciles like Beamish?" Muddiford asked me. "It's clear to me that you have no intention of killing any gods, as you didn't even kill Ozzie."

"Why should I?"

"Because: *He was sent to kill you*," Muddiford said, very slowly like I was the imbecile.

"Like I said, we'll be here when you decide you need us," Cadby stated firmly.

"So you're all just gonna stay here?!" I asked, throwing my hands up in the air.

"Yes," the Four Dogs said in unison.

"This way you know where to find us," Muddiford added, raising his nose in the air stubbornly.

It's not like I needed them to do magic. Jainkohiltzailes don't have shadow creatures. We just function as a sole entity, no furry animal accessory. But the Four Dogs were my caretakers, my guardians, and I needed them.

Me being poisoned and trapped inside a painting should be enough to stir them from Old Kunkerpot's Realm, right? Those uncompromising sons of....

"Who are you?" a voice asked from slightly behind me.

But I couldn't turn to look at her. I was quite paralyzed.

That poison had been very effective, whatever it was. At least I could still see, blink, and talk. And breathe. Breathing was pretty important.

"No one of consequence," I replied.

"Another of Diego's women I suppose," the woman half-yelled. "Frida will love this! Come on, I have to show you off to her."

She stepped in front of me, a tall woman, with wild black hair and glassy green eyes. It was Lupe Marín.

"C'mon," she said as she offered me her hand.

But I couldn't get up, or even reach for her hand. So I just smiled sheepishly at her and said "Hello" quietly.

"Oh! This is great! He's found a woman who's even more of an invalid than Fridita! This one can't even move her legs!" she declared, and laughed as she stomped out of the room.

A small white dove then flew into the room and parked himself right in front of my face, eyeball to eyeball.

"What are *you* doing here?!" he asked as he blinked at me. "And what's wrong with your legs? Stand up."

"I can't."

"What do you mean, you can't? You're the Jainkohiltzaile. You can do anything!"

"How do you know she's the Jainkohiltzaile?" a voice asked from the doorway behind me.

"It's the only way she'd survive that poison

still coursing through her veins. It's coming off her aura like a bad stench," he explained to the dark greenish-brown toad that had come into the room and joined him on the carpet in front of me, the owner of the other voice. "But you have to fight it. Fight it and stand up!"

"I really, really can't."

"Give her some time. She has to get her strength back. It's okay sweetie, Lupe's gone to get you some help," the toad explained. "Just relax for now. I'm Paloma, and this is Sapo-Rana. We're Diego Rivera and Frida Kahlo's shadow creatures, respectively."

"Well, we're the copies of their shadow creatures that live in this painting," Sapo-Rana explained. "That's a perturbing aspect of lejerdemani paintings. Every time one of you people makes a painting we all get cloned."

"True, true," Frida interrupted as she entered the room. "How many other Sapo-Ranas exist out there in all those other paintings? It just cheapens your brand, doesn't it?"

"I wouldn't say that, exactly," he said, scowling.

"What's your name, honey?" Paloma asked.

"Sylvie," I managed to say, although even talking was getting to be a bit of a strain.

Two maids pushed a wheelchair into the room and helped me into it. Frida instructed them to push the chair out of the studio, across a courtyard, and into the kitchen. Well, the Frida Kahlo that lives in this painting.

(Maple: Wait, I haven't taught them yet about lejerdemani paintings. So explain that stuff to them.

Sylvie: Me? Why me?

Maple: You're the expert.

Sylvie: I am most definitely not.

Maple: You are now. Go on.

Sylvie: Uh. Well, when a powerful lejerdemani creates an artwork it gains magical abilities. Most major artists throughout history have been lejerdemani, as lejerdemani magic is the manipulation of the universe's energy through pigments, metal, and stone.

Maple: That's not enough. Keep going.

Sylvie: As the actual author, when are you going to explain stuff?

Maple: Why would I do that when I have you to do my work? Keep going.

Sylvie: So, dear readers who I feel sorry for,

where was I? Oh, lejerdemani, gods, and various other beings can travel in and out of magical paintings. And each painting is its own world. A moment captured. Whatever amount of time it took to create the original work is played out, again and again, in a sort of endless loop.

But one that the citizens of the painting don't really concern themselves about. They live in the painting and can never leave it, for they can only exist there. And they have no real concept of time passing. Or more like, they aren't pre-occupied with time because they can't really ever die, or grow old, or anything like that.

Maple: There. Now was that so difficult?
Sylvie: Yes.)

"She's not one of Diego's," Frida said and scowled at Lupe, who kept insisting that I was having an affair with Diego Rivera, Frida's husband. Even though I kept insisting I was no such thing.

Lupe had also been Diego's wife, before Frida came along, and she was quite a possessive type of person. Even after their marriage had ended she was still jealous of any woman with Diego. Also, Lupe liked to argue. Endlessly.

"She is!"

"She isn't!"

"She is!"

"She isn't!"

"*Then just who is she?!?!?!*" Lupe cut Frida off while gesturing broadly in my direction.

"She's the Jainkohiltzaile!" Sapo-Rana shouted at them. "Focus people! I think we need to be a bit more concerned as to *why* a paralyzed Jainkohiltzaile showed up in our painting!"

"The Jainkohiltzaile?" Frida asked, cocking her head. "I've never seen one of those. Honestly, I thought it was a myth."

"What's a Jainkohiltzaile?" Lupe asked.

"The one amongst the lejerdemani who has the ability to kill gods," Frida explained.

"Why are you here?" Sapo-Rana asked. "And why would someone drench this canvas with some sort of cursed paint, which I can now feel weighing on my soul?"

"Is someone trying to kill you?" Paloma asked.

"Someone was trying to kill me with this poison. I think. But she failed, for now. As I can't be killed. I only die when I'm a thousand years old. Which, I'm not quite there yet."

"You don't look a day over 20," Lupe said,

and then she started barking commands at Frida about the dinner preparation and instructing the maids on how to help her. "We have to fill this girl up with good food so she gets strong again! Where are the chiles?! Where is the coriander and cumin??? I thought we just bought some, Frida!"

"What are you waiting for?" Sapo-Rana asked me. "Try to get out of this painting."

"She's poisoned, Sapo. It's going to take her awhile to do that," Paloma said.

"I will see what I can do," I said as I began to mentally cast counter-spells against the poison. They didn't do much, but I was able to maintain my voice, and sit up straighter in the wheelchair.

"There, that did something. Now try and get out of the painting," Sapo-Rana ordered. "You can't sit here all day and let the enemy get away."

Paloma tsked at him for being pushy, but I nodded in agreement.

I tried to cast several spells that would send me back out of the painting. But none of them worked. I felt my strength coming back, slightly. But still spell after spell didn't work.

I did feel a shudder in the fabric of this world though. A ripple in the power of its very foundation.

And I had the thought that if I really did want to leave this painting, I may have to rip this world apart to do so.

I looked down at Paloma and Sapo-Rana, who were both settled in my lap. They looked back up at me, knowingly.

"You can do it if you need to, sweetie," Paloma said. "It's not like we're the only version of this world that exists."

"What do you mean—'if she needs to?' Of course, she needs to. She needs to get back out there. Someone is trying to kill her!" Sapo-Rana explained.

"There must be an alternate method," I replied.

"Which would be what, exactly?" Sapo-Rana asked.

"I'm sure we can figure something out," Paloma said.

"Well at this moment, I'm not strong enough to cast a powerful enough spell anyway," I said quietly.

"Why didn't anyone bring me any food?" Diego asked as he walked into the kitchen, looking for his dinner, and at least one of his wives or ex-wives to prepare it for him.

"We didn't bring it to you because it's not ready yet!" Lupe yelled at him.

And that is how my new life went for several days.

Eating. Arguing. Eating again. Arguing again. Eating some more.

Well, it was several days inside the painting, but I had no idea how much time was passing outside of the painting.

"Where exactly are we, currently?" Lupe asked me during dinner one day.

"Mexico," Frida answered her.

Lupe quickly retaliated against her sarcasm with a sharp glare.

"No. Where's the painting?" Lupe continued.

"It was in a storage room inside the House of Coventry when I came into it."

"What? The House of Coventry?" Frida said and then sighed. "You mean the painting was destroyed?"

"Yes."

"How?!?!?" Lupe gasped.

"Uh."

"How?!?!?" she repeated.

"You sliced it up with some scissors," I replied.

"I sliced up my own image?!?!" Lupe asked, astonished.

"Well, that does sound like you," Frida added.

"Whoops," Lupe said.

"But it's completely intact in the Realm of Destruction, so don't worry," I replied.

"Well, we should probably worry a little bit. There's still cursed paint over all of us," Sapo-Rana huffed.

"Do you think the cursed paint is doing something to this world? To us?" Frida asked him.

"I feel a change in the atmosphere, at least," Paloma replied. "Like Sapo said, I can feel it weighing on my soul."

"What do you think is going on outside?" Frida asked me.

"A problem," I said and smiled at her.

"Then what are you waiting for???" Sapo-Rana pushed. "If you're in here, there's no Jainkohiltzaile out there, ya know. And there has to be a Jainkohiltzaile out there."

What *was* I waiting for?

Well, I was waiting for a lot of things.

At first I expected the Four Dogs to show up at any moment, as previously discussed.

But that didn't happen.

Then I hoped for Archie's arrival. Or Henry. Or Horace. Or anybody.

But mostly I waited for Ozzie.

And did stupid things like write 'therapeutic' letters to him, which I couldn't actually send off. And I dwelled on the past, and my mistakes, and how I should've killed Riot.

But clearly I hadn't seen that one coming.

And I was also waiting for my full powers to return.

"It's the cursed paint that's my problem," I said. "I'm now able to walk and move just fine. But I can't fully cast an icon. And I'm going to need an army of them to counteract the cursed paint. But that's the thing making me weak. It's a terrible catch-22."

"I wonder why anyone would do this to you?" Paloma pondered.

"Well, the God of Death who put me in here..." I began to explain.

"*A God of Death???*" Sapo-Rana shouted with a marked tone of disbelief. "But they're supposed to be so stupid! How could one of those things ever figure out how to do this type of operation?"

"That's a good question," I said, smiling at him.

"But no matter how she knew how to do this, her main goal is to eliminate the Jainkohiltzaile. However, now that I'm in here I don't know what will happen."

"What do you mean?" Paloma asked.

"Usually the next Jainkohiltzaile is born about 15-20 years before the current one is scheduled to die. But I'm not sure how old I am. So I'm not sure if one is scheduled to show up soon. And I'm not sure if one will just automatically be born if the current one is, well, detained."

"You mean, you got trapped inside a painting by a dumb God of Death? *And* you don't even know how OLD YOU ARE?" Sapo-Rana asked. "That seems like really important information to have for someone in your position!"

"I just, lost track," I said, shrugging.

Sapo-Rana made a disgusted choking sound.

"Counting from 1 to 99 is one thing. Keeping count of 1 to 999 is another thing entirely," I said, half-smiling at the surface of the table, avoiding eye contact with my dinner-mates.

I was a bit ashamed that I hadn't actually kept track of my age and when the next Jainkohiltzaile would be born. But when the lejerdemani started dying off faster than usual, I never thought that my existence and their deaths were connected. I thought it was some sort of magical disease that they would figure out how to cure on their own.

Perhaps I just didn't want to dwell on it too much because in the back of my mind I had wondered if it was just the inevitable extinction of our species. What place do lejerdemani have in this modern world? I wondered if another Jainkohiltzaile would even be born. I wondered if I was the last one.

One day I got the answer to that query when I blacked out and fell down the stairs. Well, if I hadn't blacked out at the top of the stairs, I wouldn't have fallen down them. Just so you know that much.

When I woke up again at the bottom of the stairs—with everyone standing over me, and Sapo-Rana trying to slap me awake with his wing—my body was consumed by a pulsing, stabbing pain that told me one thing: a new Jainkohiltzaile had been born.

"What's wrong with you? Are you okay, Sylvie?" Paloma asked.

"*Aaaaaagggghhhhhhhh*! I've got to go find that baby!" I screamed, and then began to cry from

123

the agony.

"Baby, what baby?" Paloma asked.

"The new Jainkohiltzaile," I whispered. "I'll be in pain until I find that baby."

"I told you!" Sapo-Rana shouted. "I told you to bust out of this painting like a cannonball through a wall, and you didn't. Now look at this mess!"

"I'll destroy this world as I go, though," I said.

Frida and Lupe gasped.

"Do it anyway," Sapo-Rana commanded.

"I won't," I said as I shook my head.

"You can't lay on the floor writhing in pain though, honey," Paloma said as she patted my head. "That won't do anybody any good."

"You said you need an army of icons, right?" Sapo-Rana asked.

"Yes. Something powerful."

"*An army?*" Frida asked as she winced. "How are we going to get a whole army of them?"

"Perhaps we need to think a bit smaller," Paloma suggested.

"Smaller? Smaller?! *Smaller?!?*" Sapo-Rana scoffed, repetitively. "Wait. Frida follow me."

He flew off out of the room, with Frida trailing behind him.

They returned and Frida handed me a ceramic Mesoamerican figure she had brought from the garden, after Lupe helped me sit up against a wall.

"We have a couple hundred of these," Frida explained. "And I can activate all of them. Will they help?"

I held it in my hands, turning it slowly. The arms were impossibly small, but its body was robust and formidable.

"Bring them to me, and a sharp knife," I answered.

Years ago during my life in Old Kunkerpot's Realm, we had a metal colander. One of its legs broke from old age, and it would no longer stand upright on its own. So Muddiford was going to throw it out.

"No, no! Give it to me!" I exclaimed, clapping. "I want it."

"What are you going to do with it?" Muddiford asked, furrowing his brow.

"I'll make it into a pet."

"You already have four dogs," Cadby replied.

"You aren't pets," I replied. "Most of the time you guys don't even walk on four legs like normal dogs do."

"True," Wooferton said, nodding.

Muddiford reluctantly handed me the colander.

Earlier that week I had learned how to turn inanimate objects into animate objects by adding a drop of my blood to their surface and casting a control spell. This also worked for animated magical sculptures, if you wanted them to do certain tasks.

I quickly grabbed a knife from the kitchen drawer, punctured a small hole in my thumb, and pressed the spot of blood against the colander.

Soon enough the gimpy little colander was shambling around on two good legs, and one extra-swingy one. In a circle. He wasn't very good at going in a straight line.

"I'll name him Nyumps!!!" I announced, grinning from ear to ear. "Nyumps the Gimpy Colander!"

"You are too easily amused," Wooferton said, and rolled his eyes.

Here inside my painting prison I would apply that old Nyumps lesson, a simple skill, to the army of Mesoamerican figures owned by Frida and Diego, and use them to purge this world of the cursed paint.

Frida and Sapo-Rana went to activate all of the figures, i.e. bring them to life, another basic lejer-demani skill. And they sent a maid to bring me a knife.

"Here they come!" I heard Sapo-Rana shout from the courtyard.

Soon enough a line of petite ceramic figures appeared from around the corner and began to march toward me. I added a drop of my blood to each one and tasked them with the OCD assign-ment of cleaning the cursed paint off the aura of this world.

This went on for an hour, until I passed out from a combination of the pain and blood loss. Paloma had been telling me to slow down, and drink something. But I had ignored her.

I woke up a few days later. Luckily, in a bed this time and not at the bottom of the stairs. But still in severe pain. Sapo-Rana delivered the news that the figures were doing their job, but not much progress had been made. I requested that the rest of the figures in the collection be sent to me. And I worked on those. A few days passed. But it still wasn't enough.

So I animated every single thing in the house

that I could animate. Día de Muertos skeleton figures. Papier-mâché figures and monsters. Mexican folk art dolls. Anything with arms and hands.

And they all worked like busy little bees, mopping away at the curse with tiny magical sponges that came with my spell. But it wasn't enough.

So I animated all the paintbrushes, and rags, and towels, and—but it still wasn't enough.

"Bring me the trash. Can you bring me all the metal trash?" I asked Frida from my bed. "From the whole neighborhood. I need to build a bigger army."

"An army of trash?!?!" Sapo-Rana spat.

"Just give her a chance," Paloma said, smiling at me.

I was going to need more than a chance.

I was going to need a miracle.

Eventually, my miracle came in the form of a small robot that I had crafted out of a mustard tin, a bicycle bell, some typewriter arms, two measuring spoons, and some nuts and bolts.

His name was Pitkin.

CHAPTER SEVEN.

A Few Words From Me.

I Am Pitkin.

By Pitkin.

Most people have a birthday.

Well, all people have a birthday, right? And animals. Those too. And plants, even. Even the Eight Great Realms must have been created on a certain day. And the planets, too. Whatever they are.

Okay. All things have a birthday. I think.

And even I have a birthday, too.

But I don't know when it is.

Sylvie made me. An odd little robot. On a specific day.

I'm not sure which day of the month it was. Or

even the day of the week. Or even the hour. Wait. I don't even know what month it was. That's the important bit, right?

I'd like to be able to celebrate my birthday one day. But when you don't know which day it is, or what month it falls in, that does make it difficult.

If you can't tell, I'm not the sharpest robot in the drawer, as there is literally nothing in my head. Well, there's air in there. So I guess that's not nothing. Is that a double negative? Are those bad?

Anyway, I often forget my own name. Even though it's written on my chest: Pitkin's Old Home Brand Pure Spices Mustard. Hence, I am Pitkin.

I wasn't really going to call myself Old. Or Old Home. Or Home. Or, well, you probably get it.

I was the 1,000th soldier in Sylvie's army of tiny workers. And I was special. Not just because my small tin body had once held mustard. But because in addition to the air in my head, the words of the Forza d'Amore were also in there.

Most of the time those words were expletives that I can't really write here. Mostly because I don't know how to spell them all. A lot of them were in Italian, Latin, Greek, Basque, Arabic, ancient Egyptian, Chinese, well, you get the picture. And I have a hard enough time remembering English.

"Try harder you dried up turd of a !@#^^&* &&^%#@% soldier!!!!" he screamed at me one day, probably a week or so after I was born.

Most of that sentence was in English, so I could understand it.

He was trying to hit me with a flaming arrow through the poisoned canvas. I could then be pulled out of the painting we were all trapped in. And the wretched poison would disappear as Sylvie's cleansing spell is released through the hole I create with my departure.

Or at least that was his plan.

I wasn't confident it would work.

Mostly because I had no idea *how* it worked.

The Forza d'Amore is the Force of Love icon and he basically looks like a naked Cupid-y type baby thing. (I could also see him in my head, slightly, as he yelled at me.)

He had been sent by Ozzie, the love of Sylvie's life, who was currently existing elsewhere as a cabinet. Well, Ozzie had sent some wind gods to go find Amore, which is why he showed up already ticked off.

Fully-cast icons only answered to the Jainko-hiltzaile and the Four Dogs of the Apocalypse. Anybody else calling them out was not a good idea. Even gods. Even Gods of Death like Ozzie.

Amore was only interested in helping Ozzie because he would ultimately be helping Sylvie. If she wasn't involved, well, Ozzie would've been up the creek without an icon. Jainkohiltzailes used fully-cast icons to help them kill gods, so the icons liked to keep their distance from said gods. Conflict of interest and all.

Anyway, where was I?

Oh, yes. Amore wants to shoot a magical, flaming arrow through the canvas, into me, drawing me out and ending our painting purgatory. Got that?

Well, we tried it about a thousand times and it wasn't working.

Amore blamed me because he couldn't really see that well into the painting, and I wasn't smart enough to figure out a better way to get myself shot.

Perhaps at the heart of the matter there was one major issue. I just wasn't too eager to get myself shot.

"The problem *is*—even though life is disappointing, you have to *keep living it*," Sylvie said to me later the same day when Amore called me a dried up turd of a !@#^^&* &&^%#@% soldier.

Well, she didn't quite say that to me. More like she said it to the room of us poison-aura-scrubbing workers. Or maybe she just said it to herself. Being confined to her bed because of debilitating pain she often talked to herself now. Or maybe it was just the painkillers she was on that were doing the talking. But I listened intently just the same.

"When I was young I wanted my life to be a big adventure. I wanted to go everywhere and see everything, and *be* everyone and everything. A different life. Something more. Something bigger. Something grander. Something different. But the world is not more. It's not bigger. It's not grander. It's not different."

At first she seemed to be staring in my direction as she explained whatever she was explaining.

But then I realized she had animated the jewelry that had been sitting on the dresser behind me, and all of the rings, bracelets, and necklaces were now floating in a spiral in the air above my head.

More jewelry floated in from the hallway, seemingly coming from every room of the house. The spiral grew until there was a swirling vortex of bling.

One of Frida's dogs came into the room to bark at the bejeweled cyclone.

Sylvie cast a spell on him and he floated over to the bed and into her arms.

He was too stunned to respond.

"Maybe the best place in the world was actually in my own home. With the Four Dogs," she continued, as she hugged the hairless creature. "My trees. The warm backyard pond. The endless summers."

She snapped her fingers and two lit candles on the nightstand next to her bed grew legs, and stepped from their holders. Then they grew arms and hands that clasped together. Music began to play. From where? I had no idea.

The candles began to perform a delicate pas de deux ballet on the tabletop.

"When I went off with Ozzie I somehow thought my life would be bigger than that house," she said. "But it hasn't been. It's been smaller. And sharper. And pointless. If I thought that place was pointless, I was wrong. If I thought being with my dogs was pointless, I was wrong. Maybe I'm just getting lost in the nostalgia of it. There were negatives along with the positives. But I know that I created a lot of those negatives myself, while I was thinking there was so much more to life than what I had in my little bubble."

She watched the candles dance as she squeezed the dog.

Tears formed at the corners of her eyes.

A doily began to float from the dresser over toward the candles.

Was she thinking about starting a fire??

"But life isn't more," she said. "The dreams I had were pointless and worthless and I regret having them. I keep telling myself that maybe the dreams I *have* achieved will actually work out in some way. *But what dreams have I even achieved?!*"

The doily hovered closer and closer to the nightstand.

"Out of the things I wanted as a girl, I only got one. And in my honest opinion, that one thing has totally screwed up my life."

The doily was now directly above the dancing candles, and it started a slow descent. *I hope that thing is flame retardant.*

Do they have flame retardant doilies in 1929?

"I mean, where is he now?" she asked. "*Where is the love of my life now?* Would I even be trapped in this painting if I had never met Ozzie??? Does he hate me that much that he just leaves me here to die? *The love of my life?!?! Sssshhhhhhiiii.* You want to mess up your life? Get one of those."

The doily stopped its descent.

"Wait, what was he? Did we ever even label what we had?" she asked the dog, staring into his eyes. "Well, he certainly wasn't my husband. I have a higher chance of getting a colonoscopy while simultaneously getting hit by lightning than getting a husband."

The dog didn't reply.

Probably a smart decision on his part.

The doily floated down onto the candles and burst into flame.

"I'll be dead soon," she said as she watched the conflagration. "And I can't even have children. Who would possibly want to marry a dying, barren woman?"

"You know," Sapo-Rana said as he flew into the

room and cast a spell to put out the doily-fire. "Jainkohiltzailes are supposed to be concerned with other matters. That's why they can't have kids and don't get married or bother with any of that mundane stuff. They have a higher calling."

"A higher calling? Is this a higher calling?" she asked him gesturing to her bedridden state.

"Is there a way I can interrupt your bizarre, pathetic soliloquy?" the dove asked.

"Ugh. It doesn't matter. It's all pointless. I long for the lovely simplicity of the past because I didn't really know what pain and disappointment were back then. I didn't understand all of the hard work and tears and anger and frustration that Old Kunkerpot probably had to go through every day just to do his damn, stupid job. Just to give me that beautiful house and yard. Just to keep me there, healthy and safe, and give me everything I ever needed."

"He did what he had to do," Sapo-Rana said.

The dove and the Godkiller stared at each other.

"Life isn't easy," she whispered.

"Should it be?"

"Maybe. *Ugghhhhh*. Old Kunkerpot must've been so lonely."

"You can't assume that."

Sylvie sighed deeply and buried her face into the dog.

"I hate myself," she mumbled.

"Um. So we can stop this now, right? Do you want some lunch?" Sapo-Rana asked, once again trying to derail her sobfest.

But the attempt was in vain.

"I always thought I'd have a better life than what I had growing up," she continued, ignoring Sapo-Rana's pleas. "But the life I wanted, I envisioned, I dreamt of—I don't have that. I can't even roll over in this bed without dry heaving and breaking into sweats. And the idea of how much effort I have to put in to get out of the bed to go to the bathroom makes me want to just crap myself. But then *that* thought makes me want to cry."

"Where exactly is this conversation going? There's only so many things I can help you with. If you need a woman in here, lemme know."

"Thinking about getting out of here and getting that baby keeps me awake at night," Sylvie continued, perhaps not even listening to Sapo-Rana anymore. "And I don't even have a way to get out. *I mean, how long have we been scrubbing away at this stuff????* God. I don't think I can muster anything else."

The doily and the candles were once again set aflame.

She is trying to set this room on fire.

"I have no more hidden inner strength," she said. "I have to keep reminding myself not to kill myself because there's no point in doing that anyway because it won't work. That's not the kind of mentally stable, balanced person who can actually get out of this painting and build the life she wants, well, for the few years I have left."

"Could you stop setting things on fire at least?" the dove asked as he put out the fire again.

"This isn't being a human," she replied. "I don't know if I ever was a human. But I haven't been one for a while. I thought I would have a better life. But I guess I was never really going to be able to build the life I wanted. My time was never really mine. My life was never really mine."

"Dear gods, how many more pills did you take???" Sapo-Rana asked her after he had gone over to the other side of the bed and discovered the many empty pill bottles on the floor.

"Just a few more," she answered. "Maybe."

"On top of the pills I just gave you a half hour ago?!?!"

"Yes. Wait. You gave me pills? When did you do that?"

I looked down at the characters on my hands, naturally there because my arms were from a typewriter.

A big W. A little w. A colon. A semi-colon. What did that even mean? Ww:;? Was there some special meaning to that? What would colon semi-colon do?

Sylvie's words echoed in my head: "My time was never really mine. My life was never really mine."

Well, I had these hands and these arms and these bolt eyes to look at them with because of Sylvie. And this was the extent of my love for her? Playing it safe and not doing my best to get shot?

I was the only one who could communicate with someone outside the painting and here I was being selfish.

I was standing in the way of her seeing Ozzie again.

He had sent Amore. He was trying. And I wasn't

doing my part.

Meanwhile she was clearly going bat crap crazy. Her level of patheticness had moved well past comical and straight into tragic.

Someone needed to put her out of her misery.

So I looked around the painting one last time, and called out to all of my soldier comrades to come to Sylvie's room and start scrubbing away at the poisoned aura in one concentrated place, right at my feet.

"What are they doing?" Sylvie asked Sapo-Rana once she noticed the influx. "I didn't tell them to come here."

"It's that little gold one. The mustard guy. It seems like he's telling them what to do," Sapo-Rana said as he gestured toward me.

Unfortunately, I couldn't actually talk to Sylvie. My magic was not that advanced. So I couldn't explain to her what I was doing. But hopefully once a hole was torn in the layer of poison she'd know what to do.

"Uggggghhhh!!! *Finally* you maggoty piece of..." Amore shouted at me, from inside my head. "I'm tired of being the only one working on this! Now stand there and don't move! I'm going to throw everything I have at you."

I felt the poison layer weaken slightly around me as all of the soldiers worked together scouring the painting's aura, and Amore worked on casting spells from the other side toward me.

And as swiftly as I had made my decision to help Sylvie as much as I possibly could, a flaming arrow pierced through the aura and through my tin body, and I went up in flame.

"For Spartaaaaaaaaaa!!!!!!" I screamed as I disappeared and reappeared in a huge room made of vines, its walls hung with other paintings all covered in cursed paint.

Amore was also there, floating in the air on his golden, gleaming chariot of love, pulled by two lions of love.

"*What the hell?!?!*" he yelled.

"What? I thought it was an appropriate quote," I explained.

He then threw his dolphin fish of love at me.

Followed by his wreath of flowers of love.

And another flaming arrow of flaming love.

But there I was. Not really burnt up.

Not really injured.

And not really with Sylvie following right behind me out of the painting.

"*Oh. My. God,*" Amore exclaimed as he jumped

out of the chariot, and flew over to the Kahlo painting. "What do I have to do to get her out of this thing?!?!?! *Do I have to call upon other icons?* I mean, that'll just be embarrassing if anyone else has to show up and then I have to explain that I couldn't take care of this on my own. I'll never live it down."

"Well, she's dying. Time is kinda of the essence," I explained to him.

"She's dying?!?!? That means there's another Jainkohiltzaile out there already. Aagghhh, but I can't sense its presence. Dumb thing. Where is that lousy piece of...? You! You go out there and find it. She or he will be able to bust the old Jainkohiltzaile out of this stupid painting, and I won't have to embarrass myself in front of other icons."

And Amore snapped his fingers and sent me off on my way.

Except my way ended up being in a deserted, burnt wasteland. A beautiful Byzantine-style clock tower, well, towered, in the middle of it.

"What am I supposed to do here???" I asked to no one in particular because no one was here.

The door at the base of the clock tower opened and a white goose appeared.

"Uh-hmmm," he cleared his throat. "Most people come here to play the Game of Goose. But as you can see, the game board's been destroyed. Which is ironic since we exist as an offshoot of the Realm of Destruction."

"I'm confused. Just slightly. But still definitely confused. No, no. Wait. I'm really, really confused," I said.

"Here, this die will help bring you to the next Jainkohiltzaile," he said as he held up a black die on the tip of his wing. "Amore just explained your errand to me. And if you give this die to her, she will be able to come here. But the board will have to be restored, and the game will have to be played before she can get to the place where Sylvie is. I'm afraid even I can't go there myself. The game will have to take her there. Once she wins it."

"But I was just in the room with the painting where Sylvie is and all it took was a finger snap from Amore to come here!?!? Why isn't it just as easy to get back there?" I pleaded.

"To come from there to here is one thing. This place is fixed and never changes. Where the painting is located constantly changes. Like a floating island adrift on chaotic oceans. And I

144

can't get a reading on it. All I know is that it's in the game. And Riot said 'if you can't play the game, you can't win the game, if you can't win the game, you can't find the painting,' as she destroyed the board right in front of my eyes. Smiling like a crazed maniac the whole time, she was.

"I wish I could've stopped her. But I didn't even understand what she was doing until she was done. No one's ever destroyed my game board before! I mean, what's the point??? It's just a blasted game. If you see that woman, make sure the next Jainkohiltzaile takes her out. Just who does she think she is???

"If only Archie was here. Well, actually, no. He's pretty useless. Just who could've actually stopped that dreadful woman?" the goose asked as he scratched his chin with his wing. "Oh, I'm George by the way."

He reached out a wing to gently shake my hand.

"Mustard, no—Pitkin. That's it. I'm Pitkin. Nice to meet you."

"Well, take that die and be on your way. If the next Jainkohiltzaile touches it she will be brought here. I'll send you to Horace Welser's house. You can start from there. He's usually quite useful. Although I haven't seen him around lately either. In fact, no one visits anymore. I guess that's thanks to Riot. Perhaps that die is the only way in and out of this game now. So protect it well, Pitkin."

And George snapped his fingers and sent me off on my way.

Okay, just kidding.

I was trying to see if you were paying attention.

George is in fact a goose and doesn't have fingers to snap. But he does this weird thing where he opens up his wings and this warm, bright white light pours out from his body and floods over you and transports you to wherever George wants to send you.

Which in my case was Horace Welser's study.

CHAPTER EIGHT.

Tiziano's Pointy Point of View.

With Several Important Points.

By Tiziano.

(Maple: Okay. Who should we hear about next?

Archie: Wait, what was I doing during all of this?

Penny: We haven't even talked about what happened to Verbena yet.

Maple: Well, let's start with what Archie was doing. Tiziano? Tiziano?

Penny: Are you just trying to tick me off now?

Maple: Yes. Tiziano?

Tiziano: What do you want, you plebeian fool?

Maple: Uh. I need you to explain what Archie was doing. Or wasn't doing, as it would be.

Tiziano: Archie, Archie, Archie. All anybody wants to hear about is Archie.

Maple: Uh. Then talk about what *you* were doing.

Tiziano: No. And don't try to tempt me with that pointless gold star stuff. That crap won't work on me, you vile scammer.

Maple: Sigh. Alright, alright. I prepared a diamond-encrusted throne as a reward for your work. But I guess I'll have to give that to someone else.

Tiziano: Wait, wait. Hold on. Can I get my name engraved on that? And can it have a built-in speaker system?

Maple: I suppose, but only if you explain what you were doing to Archie.

Tiziano: Don't make it sound perverted, you turd.)

I sat down at the desk, next to the bed where Archie was asleep in our Venetian apartment.

And stared at him.

Probably in a creepy way.

"I never wanted to be great," I whispered to him.

But he didn't wake up.

He couldn't wake up.

At least—not yet.

So if I told him anything, everything, he'd never know.

"I never wanted to be great," I repeated. "I guess that's what I tell myself as I naively look back on the time when I first started working with Riot. I just wanted to live a peaceful, happy life. To carve out my own small corner of the universe and be content."

I took a pot of ink out from the desk drawer and shook it vigorously.

"Then you arrived on the scene and I began to reevaluate my feelings for Riot and my current life situation. I noticed I was suddenly jealous and possessive. A nit-witty childish immaturity appeared in my mind that I dislike greatly. My joie de vivre turned into sullenness, and I hate myself for that. I feel like I'm losing myself, losing who I am."

I sorted through the quills, looking for the sharpest one.

Then I dragged the chair right next to the bed to be as close to him as possible.

"I hate Ozzie," I said as I dipped my chosen quill into the pot. "I hate him for falling in love with Sylvie instead of killing her. For introducing you into our lives. For this seemingly inevitable but entirely loathsome situation."

Then I began to draw hearts on Archie's face.

He still didn't wake up.

"I noticed right away how much Riot was drawn to you. I tried to ignore it or pass it off as related to her work and her job hunting down the next Jainkohiltzaile. But as time went by, it was clearly an infatuation on her behalf.

"And I can't fault her for it. I'm the same way with her. I'm not sure I love her. But I need her to love me. I crave her attention, her encouragement, and even just a small smile in my direction. I want her to applaud me, to acknowledge me, to recognize my greatness. I'm not sure that's love. It certainly feels like an addiction. A weakness. One that makes me feel quite vulnerable and frustrated.

"I have to be great. It's the only way to get her to notice me. And in the shadow of you, Archie, no one can be great. The instant you walk into a room all eyes are on you."

Having drawn tiny hearts all over his face, I began to color them in so they were solid black.

"Just what is it that makes a God of Destruction so magnetic, so enticing to everyone around him?" I asked. "I can't figure that out. Even I can't help watching you. But it makes me sick to my stomach just the same. It has dawned on me that I simply cannot compete with you.

"I realize now that I never *wanted* to be great. I just *expected* that I would be great. I'm so much better than everyone else. Markedly more clever, well spoken, and handsome than anyone else I know. I'm simply superior in all ways. So of course I should end up being someone great. But then, there's you.

"Even if I'm a great demi-god, universally recognized for my skills and brains, a demi-god can never be greater than a god. Even if that god is as stupid as a brick, which you are. In the eyes of the world, a god is always greater."

I finished coloring in the hearts and watched Archie sleep.

Sleep and dream his life away. I smiled, satisfied.

Then I snapped my fingers and made all of the hearts disappear.

Riot had signaled for me to keep Archie occupied. So I had concocted a special batch of Hawthorne berry tea that would put him to sleep.

For every cup he drank he would sleep for one year. And he would dream about his life as if he were living it.

Every year I woke him up for one day. We went out into time to look for the painting with Sylvie and Ozzie in it, and then we'd come back and he'd re-live that day in his sleep for another 365 days.

So he felt like he was making progress in the hunt, but he had no idea how much time was actually going by. I admired myself greatly for this ingenious solution.

I had established my base of operations in 18th century Venice, traveling into the past with the excuse that we were looking for the Goddess of History, but really using the muddled timeline of Earth as a shield from anyone trying to find Archie.

And they were certainly looking for him. But if he was found and he explained what had happened to anyone, we—Riot, Ischia, and I—would immediately fall under suspicion.

Archie might be a moron. But Henry Coventry wasn't.

Riot always regarded Horace as the one with the brains, but it was really Henry who was the sharpest of them all.

From the day I met him, I could tell he didn't like Riot. And I could tell he was always watching Ischia and me with extra attention. I did my best to avoid him as much as possible.

So when the Lastangs were introduced on that dreadful Halloween—as Ischia told me about the day after the party, after I had put Archie to sleep in our apartment above the Canałasso—I had the nagging feeling that they were really created by Henry to watch the three of us.

Did he know what we'd been doing?

Perhaps. Perhaps not.

But there was no reason to take unnecessary risks.

Or at least, that's what I thought.

Riot thought differently.

After the Halloween party, she visited Horace occasionally, whenever there weren't any Lastangs around him. She wanted to find out how those new creatures worked. How they would do their job.

She eventually put all the pieces together to deduce that any living, breathing thing—be it a god, demi-god, lejerdemani, human, animal, whatever—could be read by the Lastangs like an open book. Every wrong that being had ever committed was basically written on their face the instant a Lastang looked at them.

This seemed like an insurmountable hurdle for our work. If any of them ever looked at one of the three of us, the whole story would be laid bare. And there were thirteen of them out there. Searching, searching, searching.

True, Sylvie was trapped in the Kahlo painting. So technically the Jainkohiltzaile couldn't kill us. Well, not right away. But everyone would know where she was by reading our guilt, and she would be retrieved, and that would be that.

"We have to stop," I concluded as the three of us discussed the issue in Riot's office. "We have to stop killing lejerdemani, and basically go into not-terribly-obvious hiding."

"Nonsense," Riot replied. "We just have to come up with a solution."

She had already been pondering a possible solution for days prior to her delivering the news of how the Lastangs functioned to my ears. But clearly there was not yet any solution in her hands.

"You'd have to be dead," Ischia said.

"What?" Riot asked.

"You'd have to be dead, right? I mean, they can't read the guilt of ghosts or body-less souls. Those ships have already sailed, because it's not like a ghost could be the one doing this. You have to be living and breathing for them to be able to read your guilt. So if you want to be able to avoid them reading you, you'd have to be dead."

"But how can you be both dead and alive?" I wondered. "Dead enough that they don't know who you are, or what you've done, but alive enough that you could...."

"Destroy them," Riot finished, as she smiled.

I should have realized then that this conversation would not lead to good things.

Perhaps it would lead to great things, but not good things.

A few weeks later Riot announced that she was going to kill me.

"Pardon me?"

"Well, sort of kill you," she explained. "Just swallow these little vials I've prepared, and then I'll choke you to death while I cast a spell."

"You'll what?" I asked as she handed me several tiny glass vials glowing brightly with different colors. Each had a silver chain attached to it.

"I'll kill you, but you won't actually die. Well, you'll die but you'll come back to life. I figured out a way around the Lastang issue."

"Wait, what does Ischia think of this plan? What exactly *is* this plan?"

"Ischia?"

"Where's Ischia?"

"Ugh, well I have some bad news for you," she said as she tapped her fingers on her desk without looking back at me. "She's gone missing."

"*What?!?*"

"I mean, if the Lastangs had caught her—well, they'd all be here at my door already, right? But she's still missing. So maybe she's just hiding out somewhere."

"What if she's hurt??? What if something happened to her???"

"Well, that's why I need to kill you. We need this spell to work so we can handle this issue. By the way, Ischia loved this plan. She helped me come up with it, in fact. As a key player, if you will."

"Are you sure this is going to work?"

"Of course it will work. It's another Horace Welser Special," she said, smiling. "Now just swallow these vials."

So I followed her instructions. Like I always did. But my palms were sweating. I was worried about Ischia. Was this really the only solution? Would I be able to find her after this spell was cast?

After I swallowed the eight vials, I felt something like a chain wrap around my heart. It began to burn.

Then I started having difficulty breathing and I dropped to my knees.

"Ooo! Ooo! That's it!" Riot exclaimed as she grabbed me by my throat, closed her vice-like grip around my neck, and stared at me. Her strength was astounding. I had forgotten how brutal a God of Death could be.

My heart, my blood—well, really my whole chest—felt like it was melting, as I looked back into her cold eyes.

And then I passed out.

When I woke I cried for several days.

I guess I should be ashamed to admit that, as a man.

But I was no longer a man.

I was a skeleton.

A talking, moving, seeing, skeleton.

I was both dead and alive.

Is this what I had worked so hard for?

Is this what I was to become?

Riot had assured me that I would be able to switch back and forth between my soft, warm corporeal version, and my cold boney, pointy version. But it took me two weeks to figure out how to master that spell. Two weeks of wondering if I would be stuck as a bag of bones forever. And two weeks of breaking all the mirrors and reflective surfaces in my house.

This situation caused the first small dent in my feelings for Riot, and a shadow began to grow over my heart. Even when I was just a skeleton and my heart wasn't even there. I should've recognized it for the warning sign it was.

And when I had looked into her unfeeling eyes as she killed me, I should have realized that I would never see my sister again.

(Penny: Uh. That was creepy. Is everyone else as creeped out as I am now? Did anyone else just read that?

Maple: Nope, just you and me. The other characters were occupied by a box of kittens I used to distract them. You, however, aren't so easily distracted, are you?

Penny: Um. So what about Verbena? *How long do I have to wait to read about that part?*

Maple: Well, let's see what she can tell us now. Since you're being so darn pushy, and the kittens aren't working on you. How about puppies? Will puppies work?

Penny: Go on. Write Verbena's part, you heartless moron.)

CHAPTER NINE.

Verbena's Thoughts.

By Verbena.

Thinking back I'm not exactly sure when I started saying weird things and feeling ill. But it was definitely happening by the fall of our last year of high school. That was the beginning of the end, to employ a much-overused idiom.

"Why isn't anyone here?" I asked Naomi one day when she woke me up to get ready to go to school.

"Who should be here?" she asked me, perplexed. "Penny's downstairs. So is Tom and all those fuzzy buttholes."

And then I just looked at her blankly.

I had no idea why I had asked her that question.

And I had no idea who should be here.

A different day I collapsed on the living room floor. The blood rushed into my head like I was hanging upside down and anger burned through my veins. All I wanted to do was punch someone. The feeling made me want to break everything in the room and scream at the top of my lungs.

I struggled to get up and drag myself to my bedroom for some rest.

I buried my head under some pillows and closed my eyes, trying to force the feeling to go away. But an image appeared in front of my closed eyes. Against the blackness of my eyelids, a skeleton stood. He reached out his arms and scratched his boney fingertips down over my eyes, leaving trails of blood.

Terrified, I snapped my eyes open and looked for the skeleton. I felt like he was somewhere in the room. I blinked once, twice, three times. But there wasn't any skeleton here. I touched my eyes to see if they were really scratched and bleeding—but there was nothing wrong with them.

Sweat poured down over my forehead and I felt even dizzier than before. I sat up on the corner of my bed as my stomach and throat tightened to the point of sickness. But I didn't throw up. I just felt like I was going to. For hours.

By the next morning these feelings had disappeared, but the following week they returned, and they would appear and disappear for the next month without rhyme or reason.

I only managed to go to school one or two days of each week. My grandmother had started staying home during the day to keep an eye on me, but no one could really figure out what was wrong. Our family doctor diagnosed me with 'stress-related illness.'

I hadn't really ever thought of myself as a stressed person—but the morning I woke up already in the bathroom, looking into the mirror, and pulling out all of my eyelashes—I decided that I would take a year off of school before I went to college.

I had been thinking about where to apply. I had been thinking about my SAT scores and my GPA. I had been thinking about whether I even wanted to go to a human university. Was there a point to that? I hadn't been thinking of boys, or dates, or movies, or clothes like Naomi and Penny. I hadn't been distracted by that nonsense. But perhaps that was just their way of dealing with the pressures of high school?

As I looked at my eyelash-less eyes in the mirror, I came to the conclusion that I must *really* be stressed, and that I had never learned how to deal with it properly.

But was that really all that was going on with me?

"I think there's something wrong with me," I said to Grizz later that same morning.

"Of course there is! You've developed some sort of weird allergy to breathing or something. I mean, really. What the hell is wrong with you? *Waaaa-wait*, what the heck did you do to your eyes?!?!?"

"No, I mean, I'm stressed and everything, but I think there's something *wrong* with me."

"Well, there is now. How can you go to school without eyelashes??? Well anyway, today I told Naomi to explain to everyone at school that you have a terrible case of diarrhea and you've been exploding into the toilet all weekend long," he replied, smiling gleefully.

"It's not diarrhea. Thank you for that, though. Honestly, I feel like I'm going insane. My brain, my brain isn't working right, and I keep having these visions of a skeleton."

"It'll be okay. Nothing really exciting ever actually happens to you, remember? You're just a boring sack of boredom. And diarrhea."

I smiled at him but that feeling of violent anger crept back into my mind and I suddenly wanted to smack the tiny jerboa, and scratch his face until he bled. A pain shot across my skull and landed with a terrible ache in my eyes.

"Oh, wait. Now you look weird," Grizz said to me as he hopped onto my lap and studied my face. "And it's not just your lack of eyelashes...."

I'd never really felt like hurting anyone before. Never mind my own shadow creature, who would've just spent the next 48 hours torturing me if I ever tried to do anything to him.

So this felt very odd.

I wanted to hurt someone for absolutely no reason at all. Why?

"Something is really wrong, really, *very* wrong with you," he said, looking into my eyes.

"That's what I've been trying to tell you."

"No, really—you look like you're half-dead."

"What?" I asked him.

"I'm not using the saying 'you look like you're half-dead' like when someone is ill. I mean you genuinely look like you're half-dead."

"Don't worry. It will stop soon," my voice said

to Grizz. "It's almost over."

But it wasn't me who said it.

"Huh," Grizz responded. "Yeah, I'm sure it will stop soon. But I'll just let Henry know what's going on."

And he hopped off my lap and disappeared, probably on his way to find my grandfather.

I sucked in my breath and panted a little bit with panic. Those hadn't been my words coming out of my mouth. Someone else had been talking. Someone else had been thinking in my head, using my voice.

The next day I found myself sitting on the garage floor next to the bodies of my parents, and my grandmother.

Rose petals were strewn across the floor, caught in splashes of blood. I think it was my parents' anniversary. There must have been a bouquet. What had happened here?

Had I done this?

I couldn't remember a single thing that had led up to this moment.

I looked down at my hands. They were covered in blood.

I wanted to cry but no tears would come out.

I called out to Grizz in my mind. This usually resulted in him showing up two seconds later, and spitting in my face as a greeting. But I couldn't feel his presence anymore.

"How'd you steal my shadow creature?" I asked—to who? Myself? Who was I asking that question?

There was no one else in the garage.

"I want to be what I was," I said out loud. To myself again.

Why did I keep doing that?

"Round and round we go, but now this is over. Leave me alone," my voice replied. "I have work to do."

But it wasn't me who said it.

(*Penny has left the chat room*

Maple: Well, she wanted to know about Verbena. Anyone else there? No? Just me, my own warped mind, and the readers? Okay. I guess I'll just move on then....)

166

CHAPTER TEN.

An Analysis of When Girolamo Was Archie and Archie Was Girolamo.

And When Archie Was Also Suntsitzea and Girolamo.

And Was Also Archie.

By Archie.

Hello readers.

Archie here.

So some stuff happened to me. Which is why I'm a cat at the beginning of this book. Maple asked me to give you my point of view on that stuff, and to deliberate on the past or something.

Honestly, I'm not very eager to describe what happened because it leaves me looking quite stupid. But according to Maple you need to know about it.

So here it goes....

First point: I am Girolamo.

Yes, that dude in Venice in the first book.

Some of you probably figured that one out already since Girolamo was with Tiziano looking for a painting. Which is what I was doing. Or what I thought I was doing.

I wasn't going by 'Archie' in Venice because no one in 1781 Venice is called Archie. Also, if Tiziano went around calling me Suntsitzea, that would've been equally weird.

Second point: I was asleep for almost ten years.

I discovered this fact after our encounter with Stella. Once I was able to have an actual conversation with Tiziano, which couldn't happen until I cast a spell to fix his broken jaw. I didn't like most of what I heard in that conversation. But I'll get back to that part.

Third point: I was Girolamo, and then I became that cat that showed up in the museum.

So I guess I will now have to tell you how that all happened.

But it's going to take awhile, so you should probably go get a drink and snack. And maybe take a bathroom break, too.

The Part of This Story Where Archie is Really, Really Dumb – As Presented By Archie

Well, I'll probably be really, really dumb in other parts of this story. So I think using that heading here kind of gives a false impression that I'll have everything figured out for myself at some point, and then I will be a genius. Which I'm not sure will ever happen. So just take that caveat with you as we move forward.

"What the hell was that?!?!" I asked Tiziano after I fixed his jaw with a quick-healing spell.

"Ugggghhhhh," he groaned as he sat down on the stairs, rubbing his face.

I had brought us back to the House of Coventry, to the main entryway of my house.

"Shiiiissshh"—was his only response.

"You do realize that I can kill you, right?" I asked, stepping toward him. "Now tell me, *what the hell was that*?"

But he snapped his fingers and we were transported to a room set in the middle of the dense branches of a tree.

"Oh god," I whispered.

"Ahaha. That's right," he said. "The Dragon

Blood Tree! Your one weakness."

"I'd call it more of an allergy."

"An allergy? An allergy?! You lose the ability to use your powers whenever you are near one, or even near its sap. *An allergy?!* I think it's a bit more severe than that," he said, and then laughed in a bizarre way.

"How'd you learn about this?"

"Horace. He tells Riot everything. Such a dumb twit. Please, have a seat," he said, grinning as he cast a spell that sent me flying into the chair in the center of the room. Which was carved out of the tree. So that didn't really help me.

"What's going on here? Why did you want to kidnap that girl?"

"Riot wants her."

"Why?"

He stared at me but didn't respond.

"*Where are Sylvie and Ozzie??*" I growled.

"I don't know why you're bothering to growl at me. You're not scary. I mean, you threatened to kill me a few seconds ago, and I found it quite —hollow. Archie killing someone? Pssshhhh. You are the *weakest* God of Destruction. It's pathetic. Truly pathetic. I've never even seen you kill an insect. But me. Me. Me? I can kill. I have killed.

Many people. And I can kill you."

"You can't kill me."

"That's where you're wrong. Wrong, wrong, wrong. Once again. My friend. Because Riot, with the help of half-witted Horace, figured out that the only way for a non-Jainkohiltzaile to kill a god was to un-god that god."

"You've lost me."

"Of course I have. You're playing a losing game after all."

Just then Riot appeared.

She glared at me.

"Ugh. They say that beating yourself up over things, being mad at yourself, etcetera, isn't helpful," she said. "But I'm quite upset that it has come to this. I didn't want this to happen. And I do feel like beating someone."

She looked at Tiziano.

"Don't look at me," he said. "When I tell you what I've just discovered, you'll want to kiss my feet. Not beat me up."

"And what is that?" she asked.

"What you're about to tell her—don't," I said. "Don't."

I had a feeling that Riot shouldn't know Stella exists.

"Do you think your words have any effect on me?" he asked, looking at me like I was used toilet paper.

"What is it? What have you discovered?" she asked with impatience.

"I've found the next Jainkohiltzaile," he said and smirked.

Riot gulped, loudly.

"Yep, that's right. While we were off doing that stupid stuff in Venice to distract Captain No-Brains over there, I found her. She just stumbled right in front of us. Like a royal ignoramus."

"What's her name? *What's her name?!*" Riot pressured him as she quickly crossed the room to stand directly in front of him.

"Stella," Tiziano said.

"*Stella?!?!*" she yelled as she went to slap him, but stopped herself short. "*No last name? Really?* What's that going to do for me?"

Tiziano winced but stood his ground.

"I'm pretty sure she had Valcanover blood in her," he said. "I could smell it."

"Wait, wait," Riot interrupted him. "She was in Venice in 1781. How is she the next Jainkohiltzaile then? Sylvie wasn't anywhere near 1,000 in 1781."

"She showed up with an Apollo statue," he explained. "I'm pretty sure she time-traveled there just like us. She had sneakers on. Modern sneakers. Perhaps even from the future. Well, our future anyways."

"So the important question is—is she alive right now?" Riot pondered.

"But Sylvie's not 1,000 yet," I said.

"She might be," Riot replied.

"Yeah, I kinda put you to sleep for a decade," Tiziano said.

"*What?*"

I must admit I was shocked.

I thought only a few days of painting-searching had passed.

"He's very good with teas. And poisons. And poisoned teas," Riot explained while gesturing toward Tiziano.

"Thank you, thank you," he said as he bowed.

"And he also helped me come up with this Dragon Blood Tree Room just for you."

"Why do you guys want the next Jainkohilt-zaile?" I asked.

"Well, you do remember what Ozzie was supposed to do to Sylvie, right?"

"What do you mean?" I asked.

"Originally, back when everyone still had their proper sense, Ozzie was sent to kill Sylvie *before* she became the next Jainkohiltzaile," Riot explained.

"Yes, but she was already the Jainkohiltzaile," I said. "Oh my god...."

"Oh! Look! He's finally figured it out!" Tiziano exclaimed as he slapped his leg. "Yes, we're trying to kill the next Jainkohiltzaile."

I was stunned into silence.

I hadn't expected that.

"And that's why we've been systematically killing off all of the lejerdemani. So we can finally get rid of the next Jainkohiltzaile. And now we finally, finally have that chance," Riot said.

"*You've been what?!*"

I couldn't even fathom my own thoughts.

"So it's been you guys who..." my voice trailed off.

It had been in front of us—in front of me—the whole time.

And I missed it.

And all of those people died.

And I missed it.

Riot walked across the room toward me,

watching me like a hawk the whole time.

"Honestly, it disgusts me that I'm in love with you," she said, bending down to face me, nose to nose. "I'd love to say that I *was* in love with you. And I'm not anymore. But that would be juvenile. I'm adult enough to admit that I'm still in love with you. Despite our clear inability to ever be together. Especially now."

My facial expression was definitely one of horrified surprise.

Tiziano's facial expression was definitely one of anger.

"But there's just *something* about you," she said and sighed, looking longingly into my eyes.

"I'm pretty sure he has scabies," Tiziano said and coughed.

"Scabies?" Riot asked him. "Nice try. Gods don't get scabies."

"Alright, then rabies," he offered.

"We don't get that either. I would tell you to leave, Tiziano. But I kind of need you here to do your job. So how about you just shut up?" she asked him.

Tiziano coughed again as a sign of acceptance.

Then she went back to staring me down, nose to nose.

"I've often asked myself—if you were mine, would that be enough? If you were mine *would* that be enough?"

Was I supposed to answer her?

She continued to stare at me, seemingly pondering her own question.

"I..." I began to say something.

I wasn't sure what I was going to say though.

"If I gave you a hundred, no—*a thousand kisses* —do you think you'd fall in love with me?" she asked as she looked down at my lips.

I glanced over at Tiziano.

Judging by his facial expression he was either about to cry or poop himself.

"Are you trying to seduce me?" I asked as I looked back to meet her gaze.

"Am I? I wonder."

She stood up straight and walked away from me, clicking her tongue as she walked. She never once looked at Tiziano, who had been boring a hole into her head with his piercing stare.

"Well, I'm pretty sure Ischia kissed you a thousand times. Or at least tried to. And that didn't seem to make you fall in love with her. So perhaps that won't work," she said.

"Love..." I once again started to say something, but I once again had no idea where I was going to go with it.

"Do you think love matters?" she interrupted me.

"Why wouldn't it matter?" I answered with a question of my own.

Where was this bizarre conversation going?

"Love doesn't matter," she stated. "I've figured that out. Some people live for their job. They live as if their job is the only thing that matters. Some people say that's me. Other people live for love. Like Ozzie and Sylvie. They lived for love. Whatever love is."

She paused and smiled at me.

But it was an unsettling smile.

"I am *in love* with you. But it's more stupidity than love, really. And I'm just not a person who can live for love," she said, nodding. "What do you live for, Archie?"

"I...."

"You probably don't know," she continued. "I've watched you and you're quite clueless. I'll tell you something though, neither love nor a job matter at all. As delicious as you look—and you are gorgeous in an arresting way, it's almost debilitating to even look at you—love doesn't matter. You know what the true meaning of life is, Archie?"

She walked back toward me, reached forward, and trailed her fingertip across my throat.

"It's power," she said. "Power is the only thing that matters. One has to have power. More power than anyone else. Much like I have power over you right now. That's the only thing that matters. In this moment. And forever."

"Does power matter if you don't have love?" I asked her.

"Well, it certainly matters to me," she replied. "Very much so. But even more importantly, does love matter if you don't have power? You can have all of the love in the universe, but if you don't have the power to control your own destiny, to keep and nurture your love—well, then it's pointless, isn't it? Because you'll just end up like Ozzie and Sylvie. Separate. Alone. Pathetic."

"What exactly did you do to them?"

"Ugh. Tiziano can explain all of that to you later. How about, I'll grant you three wishes before I kill you," she said and smiled.

I frowned at her, very confused.

"Okay, okay. I won't actually grant you anything. I just wanted to see the look on your face when I said that. I mean, I can't *actually* kill you. Can I? You're a god and all. Or can I?

"You see Horace and I had a little conversation. How do you kill a god if you aren't the Jainko-hiltzaile? Hmmmmm. You can't, right? Well, what if you somehow devised a way to stop that person from being a god? Then he could look death in the eye just like a mortal. So all we have to do now is take your godliness away."

"My what? How?"

"Start your work, Tiziano," she said. "I'll look into this Stella Valcanover thing and come back when I know more."

With a snap of her fingers she was gone.

"From here on out, things are going to hurt," Tiziano said to me.

I answered his statement with a blank expression.

I honestly wasn't sure how to respond.

A whole world that I had been unaware of was opening up before my eyes, poisoning everything that had happened in our collective past. Our carefree years together had never been carefree. There had been an agenda playing out right beyond my scope of vision. I had been stupid. Wait, I was still stupid. I *was* the one sitting inside this tree I'm allergic to.

"Also, you should know I never hated you," he continued. "Okay, that's a lie. I do hate you. *So much*. You stole my Riot's heart. But what I'm about to do has nothing to do with that hate. Well, not exactly."

I squinted at him.

He had definitely lost me.

"*Your Riot*?" I asked him.

"Yes, *my Riot*. I've been in love with her since I started working for her," he said and sighed.

"*You have?!*" I asked, with a marked incredulous tone.

"Yes, I have!" he whined.

I was surprised anyone could love Riot. She was—cold—to say the least. I had never seen her perform one act of kindness, gentleness, or generosity the whole time I had known her. She just sat back and observed life happening around her. But she never helped anyone or grew close to us.

"But here I am standing in front of the man who has engaged her gaze for the last several hundred years," he said, glaring at me. "And yet he's never looked her way once. *Do you even know what love is?*"

I continued squinting at him.

My brow was going to be permanently furrowed at this rate.

Where was *this* conversation going?

"I have no idea what's going on at all," I said. "But besides who loves who, or what love is, what happened to Sylvie? Did you do something to Ozzie?"

"Do you really want to know?"

"Why would I ask these questions if I didn't want to know?"

"Well, Riot turned Ozzie into a cabinet. And she trapped Sylvie in a cursed painting, and then hid the painting inside that ridiculous Game of Goose thing you guys played all the time. Then she destroyed the game, trapping Sylvie inside it forever, until she dies."

"Until she dies...." I repeated in a whisper.

"At which point, she'll be dead. Dying does that to people. And then she'll no longer be a threat to us. The existence of that Stella creature-girl-thingy is a good indication that Sylvie is on her way out of the picture. Metaphorically that is. She'll be in that painting forever. Well, as a corpse. But you probably understand all that. Have I mentioned that I hate you?"

"Not within the last five minutes, no."

"Well, I hate you."

And then we just continued to glare at each other.

Tiziano's glare was definitely one of dislike.

Mine was just angry bewilderment.

"And I've been asleep for ten years?"

"Give or take a few days. Yes, mostly asleep. But anyway—like I said—this next part is going to hurt, but bear with the pain. I just made this batch, so it's a little hot...."

He snapped his fingers and a bone goblet appeared and floated down into his hand. He held it over my right hand and poured a steaming hot liquid onto my skin. Then he trailed the stream up my arm to my shoulder, and it burned through my shirt as it went.

I would say I've had less painful experiences.

But I just grit my teeth.

I don't like screaming or crying.

I don't see much point to all of those dramatics.

"I do like this poison I've made for you. I know the pain is excruciating right now, even though you haven't even flinched once. I admire your strength. I can't wait until it's mine," Tiziano said.

"What do you mean?" I asked.

"This poison transfers your powers into me."

"What? That's not even possible, unless...."

"Unless you have the blood of a hundred lejerdemani to fuel the spell?" he asked, smiling at me. "Luckily, we have all of that, and much more at our disposal."

"I thought that was a myth. A rumor. Like an old fairytale."

"Oh, no. It's a real thing. It's just very old, dark magic that no one has been using for quite some time because it became, well, impolite to kill off a hundred lejerdemani just for one spell. Plus, gods don't exactly like to advertise that this kind of poison can exist, for obvious reasons.

"And it's very difficult to cast this kind of spell on a god who isn't willing. You usually only do it if said god *wants* to lose their powers and give them to someone else. But luckily you have this tree issue, which is very helpful to me."

"And what exactly is the point of this?" I asked.

"I will become the God of Destruction. You will be killed. Then I don't have to think about you anymore. *And* you can't stop us from killing Stella. So many problems solved at once!"

"Who exactly wants Stella dead?"

"The Bosses."

I rolled my eyes.

The Four Gods of the Apocalypse.

"Who else would want the Jainkohiltzaile dead?" he continued. "Gods, of course."

As the poison sunk into my skin, or rather burned its way down into it, I could feel my powers vibrate within my soul. The Dragon Blood Tree was doing its job well. I couldn't counter any of Tiziano's work. I couldn't get up from the chair. I couldn't protect my skin from the poison.

And when Tiziano drove a bone knife into my hand, I couldn't stop that either. It sunk right through my flesh, grazed my bone, and pierced the wood of the chair.

Then he took an identical knife and shoved it into his own right hand.

"*Eta orain, zer da zurea nirea da*, and now what's yours is mine," he said, finishing the casting of the spell.

The only thing in my favor in this whole scenario was that Tiziano and Riot had planned to execute me on my own turf. The Dragon Blood Tree that we were housed in was in the Realm of Destruction. I could feel that in my soul, despite not having been the one to transport us here. I know when I'm in my own Realm, and when I'm not.

And while we were here the Realm itself would work very hard to prevent me from unwillingly transferring my powers to someone else. It was 100% impossible for me to lose 100% of my powers while I was in my own Realm.

Apparently Horace had not told Riot that piece of information. If he had known it at all. It wasn't exactly well-known intel, as very few gods have their own realms.

And I wasn't about to explain this issue to Tiziano.

So I wasn't actually in danger of losing my godliness and being killed off. At least not as long as I was still in my own Realm. But I still needed to come up with a plan to break out of my tree prison and stop Riot from killing Stella. And I needed a plan to find Ozzie and Sylvie.

But there was one major problem.

I really, really suck at coming up with plans.

CHAPTER ELEVEN.

The Breaking of Tiziano.

As Told By Tiziano.

(Maple: Alright Tiziano. Back to you. Explain what happened next.

Tiziano: Why do you insist on making us talk about the most horrific parts of our lives? Can't someone else write about this part??

Maple: No. Go on.

Tiziano: I'll get you back for this. Someday. When I figure out how.)

Weeks went by, but very little of Archie's power drained into me. The poison and knife spell should've worked much faster. I spent all of my time right next to him in our lovely treehouse to help boost the spell's effectiveness. But all that seemed to do was make me crazy.

"The spell is slow in transferring his powers to you because of the tree's effect on him. We just need to be patient," theorized Riot.

"Wouldn't the tree be helping us though? I don't understand. Plus, patience isn't going to be of much use to me," I whined. "I'm spending so much time with this guy that *I'm* beginning to fall in love with him. *What's with this guy? Honestly?!*"

"Propinquity," Archie said, half-smiling.

So I decided that I needed to turn him into something other than his super-attractive manly self. To preserve my own sanity, or what was left of it.

I finally succeeded in transforming him one day when enough of his power had transferred over into me.

But I only managed to turn him into a grey tabby cat with minty green eyes. Not the disgusting, flea-covered rat I wanted him to be.

How???

Why???

Why doesn't anything ever go the way I want it to???

"God! You're even beautiful as a cat!" I exclaimed, barely managing to stop myself from slapping him.

He *was* a cat now.

It would be ridiculous for a grown man to slap a cat.

"Do you think I'll get hairballs now?" he asked me, as he looked down at his furry arms and paws.

"*Why aren't you more perturbed by any of this?!?!*" I shouted.

"I don't perturb easily."

Just then Riot appeared, panting.

"I think I've found Stella's mother," she huffed as she dropped her geomancy board onto the table. "But Horace has been keeping her in a house in the woods down the hill from his cottage. I don't know why."

"Do you think he knows what we've been doing?" I asked.

"I've recently had my suspicions," Horace said as he suddenly appeared.

Without missing a beat, Riot grabbed the bone knife from the table, lunged toward him, and stabbed Horace in the heart.

He tumbled to the ground as she cast several

death spells.

Archie yelled in anger and struggled to get up from his chair. But he was unable to do anything thanks to the tree and my spells.

"You're going to need to try harder than that!" Riot said, laughing at him.

But wait. I needed Horace alive.

"*What are you doing?!?!*" I pleaded with her as I ran over to him and knelt down. "You said you were going to have him help us find Ischia. How are we going to do that if he's *dead*?!?!"

"Leave him be," she ordered. "Let him die."

"*What about Ischia?!*" I insisted.

"Ischia??? *Ischia?!?* She doesn't matter anymore," she said, now laughing at me. "We aren't going to find her. And we can't have him leaving here alive. Ugh. How'd he track me? God, I have to go take a shower. He probably put some tracking pigment on me. Tricky bastard."

She rubbed and wiped at her clothing and hair with her hands.

"Wait, wait. What do you mean? 'We aren't going to find her?' Why do you say that?" I asked.

"We aren't ever going to find your sister because she's dead. I killed her and her soul is in one of those vials inside of you," she said, sighed and rolled her eyes. "You'd have figured that out by now if you weren't so intent upon being stupidly jealous of Archie."

"*She's what?!?!*" I asked.

"Dead. Really dead. Not coming back. Now I have to go," she said.

She snapped her fingers and disappeared.

I looked down at Horace as his life drained out of his body, and his soul drifted off to join the others in Riot's second ledger. Where she was probably writing his name as I tell you readers about this.

"Stop the death spells!" Archie screamed at me. "Block them. Do whatever you can to counter them!"

"I can't counter my own Master's spells," I explained. "It's technically impossible."

"But you're half of me now—try it!"

I held Horace in my arms, kept very still, and tried to counter what Riot had cast.

But nothing worked. No matter what I tried or how I tried it.

I'd need a fully stocked laboratory and at least seven days in order to concoct a healing tea powerful enough. And he didn't have that kind of time.

"He's really gone," I said. "I can't do it."

Archie swore and struggled to get out of the chair.

Which he didn't manage to do.

I guess this is what he looks like as a perturbed cat.

But wait. Was my sister really gone?

I bit my lip so I wouldn't cry in front of Archie.

Then I stood up and transformed into the skeleton for the first time in front of Archie. He whistled, in what I can only guess was alarmed astonishment. But said nothing.

I took hold of the eight tiny vials that hung from my spine down into my ribcage, delicately rolling them back and forth in my boney hand.

I listened very carefully. Perhaps her soul would speak to me.

But I heard nothing.

I tried to sense Ischia's aura from one of the vials by poking at each one gently with my finger.

But I felt nothing.

I walked over to Archie and stood over him.

He stared at me intently, examining my skeleton form.

"And I thought this spell on me was painful,"

he said. "This must have been ten times more agonizing."

"Riot had to kill me first to get to work," I replied.

"How nice of her."

"Is she really there? Is Ischia really in one of these things? Can you tell?"

"Can I touch them?"

"Fine, but don't do anything stupid. And don't make any sudden moves."

He reached up with his tiny cat paw and cautiously touched each vial.

"Well?" I insisted. "Is she there?"

"She's in the pink one," he said with tears in his eyes.

A sharp feeling of anger burst through me and I wanted to punch someone or stab them or break down the walls of this room. But I couldn't risk Archie escaping and then murdering me.

So I concentrated my energy on standing very still.

"She lied," I whispered as I held the pink vial in my hand. "She lied to me."

I turned and walked away, transforming back into my flesh and blood body, and then I sat down at the table.

"Oh my dear feline, now I know what a lie really is," I said, laughing—mostly to myself.

I tapped the geomancy board Riot had left behind.

Horace was still on the floor, quite dead. And useless. Unfortunately.

"Do you have any idea of how to get my sister back?" I asked Archie.

I knew this was going to be a dead-end. Asking my prisoner, who I had been gleefully torturing with burning poison for weeks, to help me. But I might as well try.

"No," he answered. "I was never very good with dark spells like that. I think she's really gone."

"Huh. Well, no wonder I couldn't tell where she was. She was right here inside of me the whole time. How could I be *so stupid?!?!*"

I slammed my fist against the table, and then we sat in silence for several minutes.

"Now I know what a lie *really* is," I repeated. "Ozzie and Sylvie are stuck in a painting stolen by the Goddess of History. Blah. Blah. Blah. Lie. Lie. Lie. Meaningless. Stupid. Pointless. *This*. This is a lie. That was just child's play."

My chest grew heavy and my thoughts clouded

over. I strained to swallow down my emotions, blinking the tears away. The shadow I had felt growing over my heart now took firm hold of it.

"And I know that my love for Riot is dead. Quite dead," I added, and fake-laughed. "How could she do this to me? To Ischia? How could she—well, this is quite the remarkable feeling, really. I might call it, eviscerating."

I looked back over at Archie, who was crying.

The god—the man—the cat—who never cried. Ever.

And once I saw that, I started full out crying too, like a sniveling infant.

"*God!!* This is never going to work, is it?!" I asked him in between sobs. "This power-transfer spell is never going to *really* work on you, is it?"

"I can't say that there's a very high chance of it working," he whispered.

I clenched my jaw.

"*Then what's the point?* What *is* the point of all this? What was the point? I help Riot blindly until I'm more useful to her dead than alive? And then I end up like my sister in a tiny glass vial tied to the spine of some other moronic demigod?!"

I stood back up and marched over to Archie.

"If I give you back all of your powers, can you fix my sister? Can you bring her back?" I asked him.

"That's not something I can do."

"Then who can do it?"

"I don't know. No one, perhaps."

"I don't like that answer. And because I don't like it, I'm not going to accept it. Someone must know how to bring her back. Riot. Henry. One of the Coventrys. A lejerdemani. Sylvie. That weird girl, Stella. Stella. Yeah...."

"She was just a child. She barely knew how to do anything. I'm telling you—Ischia is gone. No one can bring her back."

I stared at him for several minutes, as I struggled to make my brain function despite being completely emotionally overwhelmed.

"As much as I enjoy your company—which I don't—there's not enough room for two Gods of Destruction in one Realm, Archibald. I will exile you from this Realm and block you from ever returning.

"As the Game of Goose is destroyed, you won't be able to find Sylvie. And Ozzie is here. So you won't be able to find him. And Stella—well, I'll get to her first. You just continue living your life as a fluffy little kitty, and stay out of my way."

Archie squinted at me and sucked in his breath.

"I wish I had a more refined speech to deliver to you at this moment of our parting, but I don't," I finished, nodding my head in agreement with myself.

As I cast the spell to exile him and block him from his own Realm, a smoky cloud burst forth from his paws and filled the room.

I hadn't expected the spell to go like that. But when the smoke cleared, Archie was gone. So I guess it had worked.

Now I just had to find someone who could help me fix my sister.

CHAPTER TWELVE.

In Which We Have All Somehow Become Something Else.

By Archie.

"Are you Stella's mother?" I asked the woman.

She looked like she was about to answer, but then changed her mind.

"Who are you?" she asked instead.

I had used Riot's geomancy board, which she had absentmindedly discarded on the table, to go to wherever she had been last. Which I guessed was the house where Stella's mother lived in the woods near Horace's cottage.

I was now standing in a dimly lit kitchen, next to a massive fireplace that took up one whole wall, staring at a tall, black-haired woman with piercing blue eyes. She was staring back at me, waiting for my answer.

Was this Stella's mother?

She seemed sort of familiar, but I didn't quite recognize her.

"Who are you?" she asked again.

Two seconds later Tiziano showed up.

"What are *you* doing here?" he asked me. "Oh, never mind. Where's Stella's mother?!"

He was addressing the black-haired woman who was now frowning at him.

"Isn't *she* Stella's mother?" I asked him while pointing at the woman.

"No. That's Riot," Tiziano said, gesturing at her.

"No. It's not," I said. "That's a different woman."

"Yes, that's Riot. She's inside Verbena. That's Verbena Coventry's body. So where's Stella's mother?"

"She's inside *what*?!" I asked. "Verbena Coventry? Henry's granddaughter?!"

"Don't worry, she's very much deceased and has no idea what I've been doing with her corpse," Verbena said—or rather, Riot said.

"What *have* you been doing?" I asked.

"I don't have time to explain the last ten years

to you," she replied, glaring at me. "*How exactly did you escape from the tree?!*"

"Shut up about all of that. *Where's Stella's mother?!*" Tiziano interjected.

"Me? Shut up? *For you?*" she asked.

"Just tell me where Stella's mother is," he said.

"Ugh. You fool. Look on the floor. She's behind the table and quite dead," she answered, putting her hands on her hips. "But more importantly, can you explain to me *how Archie escaped?!?*"

"*She's dead?!?!*" Tiziano gasped as he scurried behind the table and knelt down next to a woman's body that I hadn't even noticed.

I walked closer to him.

This woman also appeared to be tall and black-haired.

And very dead.

"Again, *how did Archie get out of the tree*?!" Riot asked Tiziano, getting increasingly angry.

"Magic," I replied.

Yes. I was purposefully taunting her.

I admit that.

But as I looked at the woman's body I wondered how many other corpses had laid at Riot's feet during this sick crusade. And I wondered if this latest death meant that the girl I had met in

Venice would never exist.

Riot took a step toward me, clearly ticked off about the 'magic' answer. But also clearly hesitant to engage me, even in my diminutive cat form.

"Where's Stella?!" I asked her.

"According to my reading of her aura, this woman has never carried a child. So Stella hasn't been born yet. Job complete," she said and then smirked at me. "No mother. No child."

How can I fix this? Can I fix this?

"*What?!?!*" Tiziano yelled, as he freaked out and pounded his fists into the floor. "I need that girl!!!"

"Why are *you* spazzing out so much?" she asked, as she glared at him with disgust and surprise. "This was our goal."

"This was *your* goal. My goal is to save my sister. And I need Stella in order to do that!" Tiziano screamed at her.

"Save your sister? What kind of stupid idea is that? Well, there's no Stella. There's never going to be a Stella. So get over it," she said and then clicked her tongue at him.

"*Aaaarrgggghhhhhh!!!!*" he screamed like an animal and lunged forward, clawing at her with his bare hands.

"*What the hell is wrong with you???*" she asked as she deflected his initial attack and cast a death spell on him.

He began laughing maniacally.

"*Look at you!*" he cried out.

"Why isn't…" she began.

"Look at you! *Trying* to kill me," he continued.

"Just give me a second and *I will*," she replied, casting another death spell on him.

"Ppppttttsshhh," he made a noise of disbelieving amusement.

Riot growled at him in response.

"*You've made me into a god!!!* Remember?!? You fool!! *You* can't kill me anymore!"

And he chuckled. Mostly to himself.

For the first time in as long as I had known Riot, I saw a look of genuine worry appear on her face. Well, Verbena's face really. But it was still genuine worry just the same.

"I can't kill you," she said in a small voice.

Tiziano continued laughing while he cast a tornado spell and started hurling every loose object in the cottage toward Riot.

"You can't kill me! I can't kill you! But I *will* hurt you until you *beg* for mercy!" Tiziano screamed.

He had clearly lost it.

If he had ever had it.

After the knives, forks, plates, and toaster had been thrown at her, the table and chairs started their journey up into the swirling vortex of junk that Tiziano was using to attack Riot.

She screamed bloody murder as she blocked the table from hitting her by casting an explosion spell. The table burst into a million dusty splinters.

"*You can't do this!!!*" she yelled at him, as she cast a spell to drop part of the ceiling on him.

Which he then just sent into the tornado so it would spin toward her instead.

"*I can do whatever I want!!!*" he screamed back, as he tried to grab her by the hair, after she was hit by a chunk of the ceiling, and was slightly stunned.

Was this going to devolve into a hair-pulling catfight?

Riot swiftly slapped him across the face, and blocked his hand from grabbing her by punching him in the shoulder, dislocating it.

"Okay. Maybe I can't do that!" he yelled over the din of the storm, as he clutched his shoulder, and pushed it forcefully back into its socket.

More of the ceiling fell down and was captured by either a spell from Riot or Tiziano. Then thrown at one or the other. The second floor was quickly making its way down to the first, and the windows burst as the structural integrity of the whole house began to be compromised.

I cast a spell to protect the woman's body and myself from the shards of glass, chunks of bricks, and pieces of plaster from the imploding house.

But soon I was going to be the next object thrown into the cyclone, and slammed into one of these maniacs.

So I cast the smoke bomb spell I had used to escape the tree, and disappeared with the body of Stella's mother. However, I only managed to move us from the house deeper into the wintery woods, as I had yet to recover from my Dragon Blood Tree affliction and Tiziano's mysterious power-transfer poisoning.

I touched the woman's face and tried to cast healing spells, but nothing worked.

What would happen now?

If she hadn't given birth and was now dead, there would be no Stella. No new Jainkohilt-zaile. Would another one be born in her place?

I sat on the cold ground, rubbing my head, and staring at this woman's face.

Dammit.

"God, if I had just been two seconds earlier!!!" I yelled.

I heard the shuffling of leaves under footsteps in the distance, but I couldn't see what was coming. It was nighttime and these woods were quite dark.

But it wasn't Tiziano or Riot. I think they would've both been screaming at the top of their lungs the whole way here while simultaneously destroying the entire forest.

It sounded like just one person.

I cast a spell to light up the darkness around me, and a red-haired woman dashed from behind a tree, running straight toward me. But she stopped in her tracks at the appearance of the bright light.

Once her eyes adjusted she noticed the corpse and ran to it.

"Jeanette! Jeanette!" she yelled to the woman. "Jeanette!"

"I'm afraid she's very dead," I said.

"Who are you?!? *Did you do this???*"

"I'm Archie. And no, I didn't do this."

She knelt on the ground, staring at the body. She looked like she wanted to cry but had perhaps forgotten how.

"How did this happen?" she whispered.

"Someone murdered her. But I'm confused as to how and why."

"Wait. Did you say Archie?? As in Archie, Suntsitzea, the God of Destruction who's been missing for ten years? *That Archie?*"

"Yes, that's me. How do you know about me?"

"I'm Penny Welser. Horace's granddaughter. But why are you a cat now? And who did this to Jeanette? Why did they kill her?"

"Uh, well—I—it's a long story. First, I need to confirm something. She's never had a baby? This woman's never had a baby?"

"She's never *carried* a baby, no. But she—wait, why do you want to know? Are you sure you didn't do this?"

"I don't kill people. It's not in my—well, that's not what I do."

"I don't understand what's going on here. So maybe I shouldn't tell you this, but she does have a daughter. Even though she didn't give birth to her herself. I'd explain it to you, but it usually confuses people more when I try to do that."

"Do you know where this daughter is???" I begged her.

"No. No, I don't. She should've been at the house with her mother. I was coming to get them for the party, but I couldn't access their house. So I was running there. But maybe Stella escaped?"

"She wasn't at the house, and I can't sense her presence in these woods. We need to find her and protect her. Someone is trying to kill her. I know of one method to possibly find her. But I need you to try and hide her from someone who —well, Verbena Coventry. You've got to hide her from Verbena."

"*Verbena?*"

Just then Penny's cell phone rang and clearly the conversation was not a happy one.

"I have to go," she said. "My family—they're...."

"Go. But remember what I told you. Hide this woman's daughter from Verbena for as long as you possibly can."

She nodded, got up from the forest floor, and ran back in the direction she had come from.

I was left alone again, with the woman's corpse. Well, Jeanette's body. Now that I knew her name.

"Ugh. What a mess," I said. "I should've told Penny about her grandfather. But maybe that's what the phone call was about? I don't know. What was that about? Is Horace's body still in the tree?"

I was talking to myself. Clearly I was losing it.

I looked down at Jeanette and pushed her hair off her face to make her look less disheveled.

"Well, I guess just because you aren't here anymore doesn't mean I can't talk to you."

Her still face gave no reaction.

I was a talking cat talking to a dead person like a weirdo.

"I'm sorry," I told her. "I should've been faster. I should've gotten to you earlier."

I uncast my light spell and stood in the darkness.

"I'm afraid it's a bit chaotic right now. So I can't give you a proper burial, or funeral. Or anything really. But I'll bring you somewhere safe."

Just then a huge fireball erupted from where Jeanette's house would've been, if it was still standing. Clearly Riot and Tiziano's fight had escalated, and I needed to leave five minutes ago.

So I cast one spell to put Jeanette in a marble

coffin, and another to take us to Old Kunkerpot's Realm. Luckily, no one knew about that place, besides the Four Dogs, Sylvie, Ozzie, and me.

When I arrived, Beamish was sitting on the back deck eating cereal, which he promptly spat out in surprise when I showed up.

"Crazy war over vampire cats!!!" he yelled as he pointed at me.

Wooferton, Muddiford, and Cadby joined him on the deck, sensing my arrival.

"Well, this is unorthodox," Muddiford huffed. "Haven't you heard of knocking on the front door, Archie? Or perhaps warning us ahead of time that you'll be visiting?"

"That *is* Archie, isn't it? *Are you cat?*" Cadby asked, squinting at me. "Why are you a cat?"

"Is that a dead person???" Wooferton asked, one eyebrow raised, as he came down the stairs to examine the coffin.

"There's some stuff I have to tell you guys," I said and then sighed.

"How to use trekking poles the wrong way," Beamish said and nodded.

I acknowledged his comment, also nodding in response, but I was completely perplexed.

"Ignore him," Cadby said. "He's under a curse

where he's not allowed to say anything that makes sense. He only speaks in ad slogans, magazine cover blurbs, and mistranslated subtitles. It's his punishment for letting Ozzie into the damn house."

"Speaking of coming into our house, why don't we go inside so you can tell us what's going on?" Muddiford said, pointing me toward the house.

"I'll put your—coffin—in the gazebo for now," Wooferton said, rubbing his chin. "We've never had a dead person here before, so that will have to do for now."

CHAPTER THIRTEEN.

In Which This Juvenile Story Continues.

Still From the Point of View of Archie.

Still as a Feline. Yep.

Surrounded by Four Dogs. Yep.

"You have to follow the statue," Cadby said after I had told the Four Dogs everything I knew about the current distressing situation.

"I don't understand," I replied.

"Follow that Apollo statue. Go wherever it goes and figure out when it meets the new Jainkohiltzaile," he answered.

"But that doesn't make sense. I have no idea

when Stella meets up with the Apollo statue. Why can't we go back in time to 1781 and find her in Venice and prevent Tiziano from ever meeting her in the first place?" I asked.

"Because if Tiziano never meets her then according to your story you will probably never meet her either, and then you'll never have a reason to show up here to have this conversation with us. Bringing us back to the same issue of still not having a way to get Sylvie back," Wooferton explained. "Yeesh. It's like you've never gone into the past before. Yeesh, again."

"Well, of course I have. I've just never had to do this kind of thing before. Well, not outside of the Game of Goose," I said.

"Oh, that *damn game*," Muddiford groaned.

"If you go into the past and start playing around with it, then you have no control over the future. And what you have lived can change dramatically. But you'll never know there's a difference. So the solution is to go into the future to find her," Wooferton said.

"But gods can't send themselves into the future," I explained.

"That's where we come in," Cadby said as he tapped his paw on the kitchen table. "We can't kill gods—which is lucky for Ozzie—but we do possess the Jainkohiltzailes' skill to fully-cast icons."

"So we can call Father Time?" I asked. "And he can send us into the future?"

"*My god.* Father Time? Who the heck is that? Sylvie did nothing useful around you, did she?" Wooferton huffed. "Father Time would be Saturn, aka Cronus, aka a titan, a god. He's useless to us. No, no. We have to call Horografia."

"In today's language it's more common to call me Horology. But my old name is Horografia. You can call me Oro though. Not Horo with the H sound though. No one pronounces that right and I'm tired of explaining it to people," a winged woman said. "So it's Oro, to you."

She had appeared of out thin air and was now taking a seat at the table with us. She wore something that looked like light blue pajamas, and a winged hourglass sat on top of her head. It was sort of like a hat, but clearly not something she could remove and set aside.

"I'm the icon of the study and measurement of time, and the art of crafting time-keeping instruments," she said to me as she started eating from the bowl of snacks on the table. "So most people just call me the icon of time. But that's not really the whole picture is it?"

"*Who* are you explaining this to? We all know who you are," Muddiford said.

"I'm explaining it to the cat. He seems new. Gosh. Still old, stuffy Muddiford, I see," she said and then clicked her tongue at him, accidentally spitting out a half-chewed pretzel onto the tabletop.

"Didn't you used to wear *normal* robes?" Cadby asked her. "What's with this outfit? Did you just come here from gym class?"

"I got tired of those old things. I traded them in for something new. And no, I didn't just come here from gym class. This tracksuit is what the cool girls wear. Also, I no longer carry around a damn sundial and a bag of instruments like a moronic mule. I just got a new watch, wanna see?"

And she pushed up her right sleeve to reveal that she was wearing at least eight watches from her wrist to her elbow. And then she popped a piece of gum into her mouth and started blowing bubbles in between her endless chatter.

"Also, I don't think you guys ever saw my beastie collection, especially since these haven't been made yet in this time period," she said as she pushed up her left sleeve to reveal four jeweled watches. "Each one is themed around an animal. Horse, parrot, panther, and cobra. I think the equine one is my favorite because...."

"*DO* you think we called you here to discuss your horse?" Wooferton cut her off, sighed, and rolled his eyes.

"No? You didn't? Well, what did you expect me to talk about besides my watches? I *am* Horografia, you knobs," she said, scowling at him. "What is it exactly that you want me to do? Wind your clock?"

"All six of us have to travel forward in time to the point where an Apollo statue goes back in time to Venice in 1781," Muddiford answered.

"All of you—*what?*" she asked, grimacing. "Forward in time to back in time? Whaaa?"

"There's an Apollo statue. Neoclassical. Definitely has the arrogance of a Canova. And at some time in the future he decides to go back in time to 1781 Venice," I explained.

I was honestly starting to get confused by this myself. But I was trying my best.

"And we need to go to the point when he does

that," Cadby finished my thought.

Oro blinked at us for a while with a look of worried perplexion on her face.

"Alright, I think I get it. I also think you guys are a little demented. And I should warn you, I'm afraid that time travel like this isn't an exact science. We may show up while he's in Venice already, or just after he comes back."

"You can't pinpoint our arrival to something more specific? Isn't this the only thing you do with your life? Bounce around in time?" Muddiford asked, and sighed. "If this was a limited edition watch release, I bet you could get us there with precision."

"Har. Har. Har," Oro fake-laughed and then stuck her tongue out at him, almost spitting out her gum by accident. "There is no absolute precision in time travel, especially when traveling forward in time to a moment that's also connected to time traveling to the past. In those cases, you show up when you show up."

She shrugged.

"Fine, fine. Just do the best you can," Cadby said.

"Is there anything but the best when you're dealing with me?" she asked, crossing her arms.

He just stared at her in response.

"*Begi baten keinu batean*, in the blink of an eye," Oro said as she blinked and two paper-thin clock faces dropped out of her eyes like tears, and floated down into her waiting, open palms.

She licked the back of one clock face and stuck it to her forehead. And then she licked the second one and stuck it to the top of my head.

"I don't really like abusing animals, but from what I can tell you aren't really a cat. So just suck it up," she said to me as she flicked me with her right middle finger—very hard—on the top of my head, onto that clock face.

I blinked from the pain and we were all in a plaza on top of a mountain.

Including Tiziano.

"Who's he???" Oro asked.

"Why are you here???" I asked him.

"*Uh, why are you here???*" he asked me. "You followed me!"

"What? No. We came here. Stop confusing me," I said. "I'm not following you."

"You're not following me?" he asked.

"No, you moron! You followed us!" Cadby exclaimed.

"Oh, I thought I did this," he said.

"I did this," Oro said, pointing to herself. "Me. The woman here. The woman with the time-travel skilz."

"My bear also drinks milk," Beamish added, nodding.

"Ignore that comment," Muddiford said. "Okay Archie, you seem to know who this guy is. Please, enlighten the rest of the group."

"This is Tiziano. The Demi-God of Death that I now—sort of—share my powers as the God of Destruction with," I said.

"So. You and I are linked by the spell that I cast to transfer your powers to me. And apparently it has the added bonus—or negative side effect, I haven't decided yet—of drawing you and I together. Physically. Even through time, apparently? Is that what just happened?!" Tiziano asked.

"Ah. So where you go, he goes. Oooo. Kinky. Me likey," Oro said and then she did a little shimmy dance with her shoulders and winked at Tiziano. "This only works in my mind if you guys are the same species though. So somebody needs to transform that cat back into a guy."

She gestured toward me playfully.

"Not true. Not true," Tiziano said and raised

his hand. "He didn't go where I went. Because I was off doing something. Which I was rudely interrupted by whatever this is, I should state that. And I didn't bring Archie along with me on that escapade."

"Was that 'escapade' somewhere inside the House of Coventry, which you have exiled me from?" I asked him.

"Oh. Yes, it was," he replied.

"That's why I didn't go with you," I said, shaking my head in disbelief at his stupidity.

"Well, when and where are we now?" he asked, pretending like he didn't just highlight the limits of his brainpower.

"2000-something. L.A. Museum-thingy. That Apollo is missing right now, according to my senses, but he should be back any minute," Oro explained.

"Don't tell him that!! He's the enemy!" Wooferton shushed her.

"I'm beginning to realize that the lines of friend and foe are quite blurry," I added.

"No, no. I'm really, *really* the enemy," Tiziano replied. "Excuse me while I go kidnap a girl."

"I'll make a deal with you!" I shouted at him as he strode off toward the museum's entrance.

"You're well aware of her skill level, or rather lack of skills. Do you think a split second inside the museum will suddenly make Stella into an all-powerful Jainkohiltzaile with the abilities to save your sister?"

He stopped in his tracks and turned around to stare me down.

Which was really very far 'down' because I was still a damn cat, and I was a foot tall while he was 6 feet tall.

"I thought you told me she couldn't be saved. I seem to recall that conclusion was made by some whining little kitten in the not-so-distant past," he said and then sucked his teeth at me.

"Well, let's say I was wrong. Which I wasn't. But if I was, Stella's not in any shape to help you. So a deal. I take her with me instead, and she and I go find Sylvie. And Sylvie can then try to save your sister," I said.

"And what if Sylvie is already dead?" he asked.

"Then I will bring Stella back to the Four Dogs to be trained as the Jainkohiltzaile, and they can try to figure out a way to bring Ischia back."

Muddiford grimaced at me. Probably because he knew there was no way to save Ischia. But luckily he remained silent for the sake of the potential deal, which would save Stella from Tiziano, for now.

"Fine. You make her into something that's useful to me, somehow, and then bring her back to the House of Coventry. Or rather send her to me, because you can't come back anyway," he said, while squinting at me. "But you can't draw this out for an eternity. My patience will run out when it runs out."

Very specific.

"Oro, bring us dogs back to the House of Coventry. Back to our original time. With this guy," Wooferton said as he pointed at Tiziano.

"Oh. I see," Tiziano said and then smiled. "You dogs can keep an eye on me all you want. But I'm a god now. So don't expect to be my Masters. I'm the Master now."

"This isn't really a question of power dynamics," Muddiford said. "But yes, I think we do need to keep an eye on you. Or eight eyes as it would be. I'm pretty sure you have a screw loose."

"Several screws," Tiziano said, proudly smirking at him. "Several."

As Oro prepared her eyeball-blinked-clock-faces for Tiziano's forehead and her own, Wooferton whispered to me: "We'll try our best to maintain the Realm, but don't take too long finding Sylvie and bringing her back to us. This guy is a nutter and it takes someone with marked sanity to manage that place. But just make sure you keep Stella away from Riot. That's your main priority, got it?"

I nodded in agreement.

I had a lot of things to accomplish, simultaneously, and all very important. But I was beginning to lose track of it all.

Was *I* supposed to be the one with marked sanity who could manage my Realm?

I'm not really sure that could properly describe me in this moment.

"*Byyyyyyyyeeeeeeeeeeeeeeeeessssssss!!!!!*" Beamish sang out to me as Oro flicked Tiziano on the forehead, while winking at him again, and the six of them disappeared from the plaza.

Now I had to go find Stella ASAP before Riot could show up. I'm not sure if she could figure out where Stella was without someone like Oro helping her. But I didn't want to take any chances. Even here in the future she's still a god, and that means she's still alive. It was only a matter of time before our paths would cross again.

CHAPTER FOURTEEN.

Hi, I'm Beamish.

I Like My Squeaky Pig.

His Name is Arnie.

(Beamish: And I like my stuffed hedgehog. I use him as a pillow when I take naps. I haven't named him yet. Perhaps he should be called Ben. Or Larry. Or Joe. Or Finn....

Maple: Beamish? Uh, you're supposed to write this next section. Can you focus for a minute on that?

Beamish: I like to lean my face against doorways to look dramatic.

Maple: What?

Beamish: A full home is a happy home.

Maple: What exactly are you talking about

right now?

Beamish: Did you know that there's a Norwegian artist who uses dead hands to paint his pictures? You know, like they're the paintbrushes. But they're dead hands. Where do you think he gets the hands?

Maple: You're even worse than the others. Focus and I'll give you a treat.

Beamish: What kind of treat? I prefer lean grass-fed beef sausages with mint sauce.

Maple: That was swiftly specific....)

"Where'd Archie dig up you four fossils?" Tiziano asked us once we had returned to the House of Coventry, where we were all eyeing each other suspiciously in the foyer of Henry Coventry's main residence.

"That's not really important," Muddiford said.

"Well, wherever it was, why didn't Archie's useless body drag me with him to that useless place?" Tiziano asked.

"It's a special place. Locked to anyone who hasn't been there before," Wooferton replied. "We had to establish a new rule about access—for reasons."

"Hmmm. Well, it was nice meeting you all.

Sorry I didn't catch your names," Tiziano said.

Then he snapped his fingers and disappeared.

"*Goddammit!!!*" Cadby swore. "Didn't anyone have an invisible chain on him???"

"You usually do that part," Muddiford answered, raising his eyebrows.

"I didn't this time," Cadby said, sighed and then sat down on the stairs.

"We'll just have to find him," Wooferton commanded. "He's still in the Realm of Destruction. That much I can sense."

And so it went.

For quite a few years.

We'd track down Tiziano. Magically chain him to something to keep an eye on him.

And eventually he'd break free.

And then we'd have to start all over again.

And we'd have to use more and more, stronger and stronger chains.

But he always escaped. And we always caught him.

"I'd rather spend my days trying to bind Fenrir than deal with this guy!!" Muddiford cried out one day after we had just managed to catch Tiziano and chain him to a nearby boulder.

"Ugh, Tiziano, you piece of—*why do you keep running away???*" Cadby asked. "There's no point. We'll just catch you again, and you clearly know that."

"I'm *Lontano* now," he answered. "I've decided now that I'm a god I need a new name. That way I can leave the past behind more effectively."

And then he smiled, creepily.

Shivers ran down my spine.

"My, my. You guys are just too powerful," he continued, sighing. "It's unfaltering. Where does it come from? I mean. I'm a god now. I should be able to defeat four dogs. But you're just too, too —dogged! *Why didn't I think of that one before??* Speaking of power, are you sure you guys can't fix my sister? I have no idea what you four things are, but you have amazing skills. Are you *sure* you can't fix my sister?"

It was probably the hundredth time he had asked us this question. He had shown us the pink vial that contained her soul. We had told him that she was really, really dead, and that we weren't necromancers. Well, speaking to the dead—yes, we could do that.

Raising the dead? No, we couldn't do that even if we wanted to. And I had never met someone who could. Well, not without making a crazed, soulless zombie thing. Which I don't recommend making those. They're scary. And I don't like scary things.

Where was I?

"No, we can't fix your sister," Wooferton answered him for the hundredth time.

"Ugh, I'm getting so tired. Of this. Of that. Of everything. Your enthusiasm for hunting me down is getting a little old," Lontano whined.

"Nothingness set a treehouse on fire," I contributed.

Yes. I was still under that curse/punishment.

But by now I had forgotten how to say normal stuff, so it didn't really matter anymore.

"Yes, Beamish I agree," Lontano said, fake-chuckling. "And while I have *so enjoyed* this game with you dogs *so much*, I'm getting awfully impatient for our poor friend Archie to send me my precious Stella."

"Just leave her alone," Wooferton said and then sighed. "Archie will take care of all that."

"Archie-Archie-Archie," Lontano started singing. "*Archie-Archie-Archie.*"

And then he transformed his right arm into a skeleton arm, and began scratching bloody claw marks into his own thigh with his boney finger-tips.

The skeleton spell no longer surprised me. He used it as often as possible. It did make tracking him slightly more challenging, but not impossible.

What *was* surprising was how he was butchering his own leg and he didn't even seem to care.

"What *exactly* are you doing to yourself?" Muddiford asked.

"Making sure I'm still here," Lontano replied quietly.

"You're not exactly the freshest fruit in the cup, are you?" Cadby asked.

"The Realm is getting to him," Wooferton said. "He's losing his marbles."

"Did I ever have them in the first place???"Lontano asked. "Ahahaahaa. Is this where the joke ends? Is this where I'm supposed to laugh? That was the joke, right?"

Then he started maniacally guffawing, to himself mostly.

"Are we supposed to answer him, somehow?" Cadby asked.

"I don't think that was a question for us," Wooferton replied.

And then Lontano started singing opera at the top of his lungs, which lasted for several hours.

Which felt like years.

Maybe it was years. You never know in the House of Coventry.

Time is a tricky thing here.

It exists. And yet it doesn't.

(Penny: So that's what happened?

Maple: More or less, yes.

Penny: Was anyone else paying attention to all that?

Maple: Nope, just you and maybe a couple readers.

Penny: Why do I feel like I know less now than when we started this book?

Maple: Because I have amazingly confusing explicative skilz.

Penny: Who allowed you to write books?

Maple: Don't worry. It's only a matter of time until the Literary Excellence Police show up to arrest me for crimes against humanity. Stay tuned!)

CHAPTER FIFTEEN.

And Back to Morrow in Badger's Wood.

Where She Attempts to Tell You Readers A Frustrating Tale That's Really Written by Maple the Lame-brain.

As we were finishing dinner I felt a shudder in the bubble. Just as I had when Archie, Stella, and Derek had come through it.

Penny and Eagle exchanged a worried look.

Everyone sat very still, waiting for someone to say something. Hopefully it would be the voice of an adult who knew what the heck was going on.

"Everyone felt that right? Isn't everyone already here that's coming here?" I asked.

"Yes," Penny answered. "And yes."

"Do you hear that?" Eagle asked.

"Hear what?" Penny asked back.

"*Largo al factotum*," he answered.

Was that a spell?

"Rossini?" Penny asked, perplexed. "All I hear is birds chirping."

Eagle's ears twitched as he listened carefully.

"Yes. An old recording. Probably a gramophone," he said. "Someone's singing with it. In the distance. But he's coming closer. And my neck-hairs are up. It's an enemy."

Archie left the table and rushed out the front door. We followed him out into the front garden.

Where we saw a giant frog lumbering up the road toward our house.

It had an elaborate golden carriage saddled on top of it. (This is called a howdah, in case you want to look that up.) And I could just barely make out the form of a man attempting to stand up in the carriage. But given the uneven nature of a frog's walk, he was failing.

An extra large gramophone horn was next to him, blaring out a male operatic voice. The frog-rider was singing along, from behind a beautiful Venetian mask. He was dressed to match that mask, in an outfit that can only be referred to as garish. It certainly matched the golden carriage.

But what the heck *was* he???

"Hide," Eagle said.

And with a snap of our fingers, Ellie, Nora, and I became a birdhouse, garden gnome, and metal butterfly.

Eagle had obsessed over that camouflage spell so much that I could've done it in my sleep. I guess there had been a point to all that drilling.

I crossed my fingers mentally that this guy hadn't seen us and wouldn't find us.

"What just happened to the girls???" Derek asked.

"They're hiding," Eagle replied. "I can't move. Can you? Penny?"

"I can't move either," Derek and Pu responded in unison.

"He's cast a paralysis spell," Penny said. "I'm stuck as well."

"That's Tiziano," Stella stuttered. "That's the guy that tried to kidnap me in Venice. How do we break this spell?"

"We don't. He's a god. And quite an impatient one," Archie said, sighing from inside a wooden cage that had appeared around him at the same time my sisters and I became garden decor. "I'm sure he's here for Stella."

Silence descended upon the group.

The two adults, the teenager, the two cats, and the rabbit were all stuck in place on the front path. As an opera-singing homicidal maniac made his way closer and closer.

"Don't let him know about the girls," Archie said quickly. "I don't think he knows they exist."

"What do we do now though???" Stella whispered.

"Nothing," Derek said. "We aren't powerful enough to break this spell."

"Well, well, well," Tiziano interrupted as he neared the front gate. "Archie, my friend. Fancy meeting you here!"

He sniffed indignantly in the air toward Archie.

Then he turned off his gramophone and jumped down from the carriage.

"You know, I imagined this frog would be a much more efficient and comfortable ride than it actually was," he said, cracking his back. "I will have to re-think this as my mode of stylish transport."

He strode through the gate, walking like he

was on stage performing Shakespeare.

And then he took turns looking at everyone.

"Why's everyone so quiet?" he asked.

"Why are you here?" Archie asked. "I haven't even had a chance to accomplish anything, and we agreed in L.A. that you'd give me some time. It's only been a day—literally, *a day*—since we made that agreement."

"Well, what might've been a day for you was a decade for me! A painful, painful decade! I can't wait any longer. I'm sick and tired of dealing with those dogs and not being able to save my sister. Plus, what can *you* do that I can't do better?" Tiziano asked. "Why should I wait for *you* to do something when I can train this girl on my own?"

"Sylvie has to train her," Archie replied.

"Maybe. Maybe not," Tiziano said and clicked his tongue. "Either way, I'll be taking her with me."

"Leave her alone," Derek said.

Then Pu attempted to spit on Tiziano, but the saliva just dribbled out of his mouth.

"Cats can't spit," Tiziano said to him mockingly.

So Pu hissed instead.

"Anyway, my friendly-furballs," Tiziano continued. "I'd love to stand around here chatting, but Stella and I have somewhere to be."

"Don't you dare take her!" Derek shouted.

"Are you going to stop me?" Tiziano asked.

Derek glared at him, but couldn't even twitch a finger.

"No. I didn't think so," Tiziano said. "But I can't have you pathetically coming after me either, distracting me. So let's take care of that issue first."

He took off his right glove and his flesh melted away and all that was left was his bones.

"Oh!" Stella gasped. "You were in my nightmare!"

"Yes, I did come into your dreams. I hope you enjoyed that. I know I did."

Then he began singing again.

"*Rasori e pettini, lancette e forbici,*" he belted out as he approached Derek. "*Al mio comando, tutto qui sta.*"

He grabbed Derek by the throat and continued singing, "*V'è la risorsa, poi, del mestiere colla donnetta—col cavaliere....*"

Derek tried to struggle against him, but in vain.

"Stop it!" Archie yelled, as he shook at the bars of his cage.

Penny and Eagle were both attempting to cast spells, but also in vain.

Pu was releasing a stream of angry curse words, which might have been a spell.

Stella just stood there saying, "What do I?" over and over again like a broken recording.

"Stop it!!! Leave him alone!" Archie continued pleading. "This is pointless!"

"Ah, Mr. Goody Two-Shoes, there's nothing you can do now," Tiziano said, smiling at him as Derek transformed into a cloud of white dust, which floated above his boney hand.

"That's..." Eagle gasped.

"*Tutti mi chiedono, tutti mi vogliono, donne, ragazzi, vecchi, fanciulle...*" Tiziano sang as he magically formed the cloud into a solid object— a porcelain figurine of a shepherd, which he then clasped tightly in his hand.

"What in the..." Pu whispered.

"Isn't it lovely?" Tiziano cooed sarcastically.

"*What did you just do???*" Penny asked.

"Oh, don't worry," he said, turning to her. "You're next. You can feel the effect first-hand."

He passed the Derek figurine into his left hand,

and then wrapped his right hand around Penny's throat.

"Nooo!!!!" Eagle screamed and began squirming in place.

"*Pronto a far tutto, la notte e il giorno, sempre d'intorno in giro sta. Miglior cuccagna per un barbiere, vita più nobile, no, non si da,*" Tiziano sang.

And in an instant Penny was a porcelain shepherdess.

Eagle was gone.

I'm sure my heart stopped beating.

I considered un-hiding myself to try and fight this man. But given the strength of the paralysis spell he was casting on everyone else, I knew I couldn't beat him.

Stella screamed at him in a blood-curdling way.

It had finally gotten to be too much for her.

Tears started to stream down her face.

"Don't panic, my pet," Tiziano soothed her. "Let me just set these aside and we'll get going."

He threw the two figurines in the air. But instead of crashing to the ground and breaking into a million pieces, they simply floated toward the frog, and settled down into the carriage.

"It's fine, Stella. It's all okay. Your father's okay," Archie kept repeating, trying to reassure her. "It will all be okay."

But she kept crying.

And I would've been crying right along with her, but that might've given us away to this psychopath. So I locked my jaw and hoped my sisters were doing the same.

"So the rabbit went with the woman. And the man—well, nothing went with him," Tiziano said, talking to himself as he stared at Pu. "And Archie is still just Archie. This does beg the question: who are you? You should've been with the man."

"I'm the God of Hatred of Men in Prissy Outfits Who Can't Sing Opera Very Well," Pu replied.

"I'll have you know that I—I can sing opera *very* well," Tiziano replied, after being slightly taken aback. "I'm known as the Pavarotti of the Realm of the Dead! But besides that, whatever you are, furball, you seem to be connected to Stella. So I'll take you with us, too."

And then he grabbed Pu by his tail and flung him toward the carriage.

Pu went spinning off through the air, but slowly like he was in anti-gravity chamber, eventually landing next to the figurines.

Tiziano then swept Stella up into his arms like he was about to carry her over the threshold into their newlywed home.

"Ahhhh, there we go. You see, this isn't so bad," he said to her, as he held her close to his chest. "It's actually quite pleasant, right?"

"What—what did you just do to my father???" she managed to ask.

He didn't answer though.

Instead he went back to singing.

"*Largo al factotum della città. Presto a bottega che l'alba è già!*"

He carried her over to the frog. Easily climbed the stairs on its side (despite the weight of his new burden), and gently placed Stella down on the bench seat. He then sat down next to her, wrapping his arm around her shoulders.

She clearly was still unable to move or I'm guessing she would've already been clawing at this guy's eyes and ripping his hair out, given the way she was glaring at him.

"*Ah, che bel vivere, che bel piacere per un barbiere di qualità! di qualità!*" he sang.

The frog turned around slowly to return in the direction it had come from.

"Archie. Archie. Archie," Tiziano called back to him cheerily. "I know you will try to follow me. But there's little point! Just the same though, here's a gift to you!"

He snapped his fingers and a bizarre tree shot up from the ground, through the middle of Derek's SUV, instantaneously growing, expanding, breaking apart the center of the car, and raising it into the air. In a few seconds the tree had a full web of branches, covered at their ends with large, needle-like leaves that reached upward. And the car definitely could no longer be labeled as a vehicle.

Archie glared at Tiziano in return, but said nothing.

"What? You aren't going to fight back? *You just don't have it in you anymore?*" Tiziano asked in a much darker tone. "That's right. Just stand there."

The frog plodded his way back down the road and out of sight.

CHAPTER SIXTEEN.

In Which I Am Slightly Conflicted.

By Stella.

As we rode the frog—or rather, rocked violently back and forth on top of the frog—away from Penny's house, Pu's endless stream of cursing meant that Tiziano eventually produced some duct tape by snapping his fingers.

And then he taped the cat's mouth shut.

Meanwhile, I was trying to turn and look back at Archie and the girls to make sure they were okay, but this paralysis spell prevented that possibility. I then tried to wiggle my way out of the seat, to no avail. And I tried to touch the figurines of Penny and my father, to no avail.

I could still breathe, blink, talk, and move my

neck slightly. But I couldn't do anything useful.

What would my father do in this situation?

Probably yell.

What would my mother do?

I wish I knew.

Tiziano sat back on the seat, crossed his arms, and stared at me. Saying nothing. Just staring. Making me quite uncomfortable. And unfortunately, when I'm uncomfortable I tend to talk, even when I don't want to talk.

"Where are we going?" I asked.

"Somewhere special," he said as he winked at me.

Um. That didn't sound good.

"It seems as if you and Archie made some sort of deal about me…" I continued, even though all I really wanted to do was transform into one of those dusty spell clouds and steal Pu and the figurines away from this guy. Or perhaps just ooze off the seat like a jelly and disappear into the ground. I was probably more capable of doing the latter.

"Indeed," Tiziano said as he took off his garish mask. "I was *supposed* to allow Archie to take you with him in order to retrieve Sylvie. However, even though I *usually* keep my word, in this scenario I decided not to."

"Why not?" I asked. Talking again. Was it even possible for me to keep my mouth shut?

"Hmmm, well it's quite simple really. I need you to be constantly questioning your own mortality so I can bask in the warm glow of your unceasing fear of torture and dismemberment," he replied, ending with a gentle smile.

I grimaced at him.

"When Sylvie dies you will become un-kill-able," he said, as he once again warmly wrapped his arm around my shoulders. An action that made me quite nauseated.

I tried to roll my shoulders as a subtle hint that I didn't want his arm there, but that wasn't phys-ically possible for me at this juncture. Sigh.

"But if you don't *know* when Sylvie dies," he continued. "Then you won't know when you've become un-killable. So I decided that it's in *my* best interest for you and Sylvie to remain apart. Right now, I can still kill you. So you'll need to do what I tell you to do. See? Simple!"

It was an odd juxtaposition to be threatened with torture and dismemberment by someone who was essentially hugging me like we were long-lost BFFs.

A man had never hugged me like this before. Well, besides my father. But he doesn't count. So I was thinking more about that than the rest of what he was saying.

Tiziano had grabbed me before and threatened my life. Which he was also doing now. But he was also being quite playful and flirty. What exactly was he trying to accomplish?

I simultaneously wanted to giggle myself to death, slap him, throw up on him, and beat him with his own spine.

I was slightly conflicted.

"I'm tired of losing," he went on. "I recently realized that I'm the loser in this story, and I'm *not* satisfied with that scenario. Why can't *I* ever get what I want? Hmmm? Why not? *I want to be the champion of this tale.* For now, you're killable so you have to do what I want you to do, and then I'll get what I want."

"Wait, why would I become un-killable?"

My slow brain was finally catching up.

"Because you're the Jainkohiltzaile and the Jainkohiltzaile, once he or she gains the complete set of powers, always lives for one thousand years as a sort of temporary immortal."

The whole time Tiziano was explaining this

information Pu was having a royal fit. Or trying to have a royal fit, while still paralyzed and gagged.

Which made me guess that Pu knew all about this thousand years thing, but just hadn't told me. Not that there had been a lot of free time to explain that in between Archie announcing that I was the Godkiller and releasing Pu and this guy coming for me.

But honestly, this guy was answering all of my questions within moments of kidnapping me, and my own father had refused to tell me anything for my whole life. My 'enemy' was appearing to be more helpful than my own family. Which was frustrating, to say the least, and which made me feel—slightly conflicted.

While my mind was racing in one direction of being ticked off at my father, Pu, and Archie for keeping me in the dark, it was also slowly floating down a second path. A path I voiced to Tiziano. Mostly because he was the only one here who could answer me.

"A thousand years?" I asked. *"I will live for a thousand years?!"*

The thousand-year path.

Yes, that was where my mind was now stuck.

A **T-H-O-U-S-A-N-D** years.

A *THOUSAND* YEARS???

"Yeppers," Tiziano replied friskily, as he was now gently petting the back of my head.

"That's not normal!" I blurted out. "I mean, that's *not normal*. How do you have a normal life if you live for a thousand years? Do you age? Can you have kids? Can you have a family? Do you go to college? Do you have a job? Do you just live for a thousand years as a wrinkly-old-raisin-woman once you get past 100? *Again, how do you have a normal life?!*"

"You don't," he answered, grinning at me like I had just won a lottery. But given his obvious love of misfortune—a cursed lottery. "You can't have kids. There's no family or college or job for you. You live. You die. You never become a ghost. Because you are a Jainkohiltzaile. You aren't normal."

My eyes were as round as teacup saucers, and I had no idea what to say next.

Was there a way I could negotiate my way out of this Godkiller thing?

"The good news is you can choose whatever age you want to be. Once you're trained. If you want to be sixteen, or thirty, or ninety—for a thousand years—that's up to you. You can pretty much do whatever you want. That's one of the perks. But clearly I don't want you to do whatever *you* want to do. I want you to do whatever *I* want you to do. I hope that's pretty obvious, by now."

He was now twirling my hair in his fingers.

Was he some kind of pervert?

It's not like I could fight him off anyway, still being paralyzed. But I felt the sudden need to rip his hair out of his scalp. I wish I could at least manage that.

"Well, I don't want to live for a thousand years," I said.

It's not like what I had to say mattered, but at least I got that thought out there.

"All of the Jainkohiltzailes live for a thousand years," Tiziano said. "When they're close to dying, their powers drain off into another lejerdemani that inherits them. The old Jainkohiltzaile trains the new Jainkohiltzaile, who lives for another thousand years. That's just how this goes."

He said all that like it didn't matter.

Like he was explaining why your car needs frequent oil changes or why his company's life insurance policy is better than this other company's policy.

"At least *you* have a clear system in place," he continued. "I could live forever, but I could also be killed at any moment. For you, you know you'll have the thousand years. Well, as long as I don't kill you first."

I was beginning to think that was not a bad option. Can't I just request the 'Death by Tiziano' murder package and be done with this before the insanity of a thousand years of life starts up?

But then I thought of my father, and how he'd probably be sort of, kind of, a little bit sad at my voluntary departure, or even my involuntary departure, from life.

My father. Ah yes—*that guy*. The man who had treated me like a six-year-old for my whole life, and for whom I was now responsible because he was an inanimate object sitting on the cushion next to me.

"What exactly did you do to my father? Can he be returned to his previous non-porcelain state?"

"That depends on you," Tiziano replied. "But you know, you're going way, way off script here. I had our whole conversation set up in my head to go a certain way, and you're just bouncing around all over the place, and it just isn't going how I planned at all. Why are you so stupid that I have to explain everything to you like I'm your kindergarten teacher? How am I supposed to be setting up an uneasy, but somehow friendly, tension between us when you keep asking me questions???"

"Uh. 'Somehow friendly?' Is that why you're petting my hair? Because that's just being super creepy."

"Creepy?! No, no. No. That's not what I was going for at all here! I'm going to have to rethink my tactic."

He tapped his chin.

"So can we continue talking about my Dad?"

"Wait, wait. Hold your proverbial horses. I had some stuff to do before we got to that part."

Tiziano snapped his fingers and two huge trees instantly grew up out of the forest floor in front of us. Stones popped up out of the underbrush and flew up into the air, floating around the trees for a moment, and then colliding into each other in a swirling storm. They eventually fused together to form an archway that sprung from one tree to the other, far above our heads.

"I wanted it to look extravagantly impressive, for you," he said as he looked lovingly at me and touched my chin.

I would say that chills ran down my spine, but that would be stating the obvious. Is it possible to have chills on top of chills? Chills with their own chills?

And then he winked at me.

"Still super creepy," I whispered.

He sighed, lovingly, in response.

Pu had started to gnaw through his duct tape gag. Perhaps just eating it.

Would that cause intestinal blockages?

So Tiziano applied a few more layers to his face. Do shadow creatures need to be able to breathe?

I just sat there hoping things would somehow start working in my favor and all of us would survive this.

The frog slowly shuffled through the tree-gate and a different world opened up in front of us, with a different path. Unfortunately, it was the road from my nightmare. Which led up to the huge metal gate I couldn't touch. And which never opened for me when I wanted it to.

As our odd frog carriage made his way up the

road with his odd assortment of odd passengers, I thought about how being the Godkiller was clearly not the type of gig that people would want to sign up for.

First of all, you had to deal with wackos like Tiziano, who at this moment had gone back to majestically singing along with his opera record. I think he was continuing his attempt at impressing me. Well, at least he wasn't touching my face as he sang.

If I had actually been trained to be a functioning Godkiller I could probably make his head explode just by thinking about it. But instead I had to watch as he did whatever he wanted.

Still, if I wasn't the Godkiller, he wouldn't give two poops about me and I wouldn't be in this situation at all.

My tiny brain came to this conclusion: the Godkiller was just the one who had pulled the short straw.

The short, crappy straw.

Of crap.

And then she sucked it up. For a thousand years.

While all of her family and friends died off around her. Constantly.

Yippee.

If I hadn't already been sitting, I would've needed to sit down to let this knowledge soak in.

This crappy knowledge.

Of crap.

We reached the end of the road and the burning gate of perpetual nightmare annoyance. Tiziano snapped his fingers and it opened instantly.

"*Honey, we're home*," he sang.

Pu growled in response, from behind the duct tape.

I would've growled in response, too. But my growling skilz are pretty lacking.

The hulking mass I had seen beyond the gate in my nightmare was a huge mansion, easily labeled a castle. Deep in the woods. But perched in the center of a well-maintained lawn and garden.

The frog stopped at another gate in front of the house's circular driveway. The kind of driveway you would expect to see posh horse-drawn carriages driving onto, stopping underneath the posh covered entrance to let their posh passengers disembark, poshly.

"It's lovely, isn't it?" Tiziano asked as he waved his hand at the mansion.

"Am I supposed to give an honest answer?" I asked. "Or just appease you?"

He faux-pouted.

"The frog can't fit through this gate. So we'll have to park him here," he said.

Then he picked me up like a ragdoll, and jumped down from the frog.

"Where exactly are we?" I asked him as he (graciously) put me down and let me stand on my own two feet like a non-child person.

"The Charles Schwab House, as it was sometime around 1906. A grand mansion that was once upon a time on Riverside Drive in New York," he stated matter-of-factly, hands clasped together like an uptight tour guide. "Archie and Henry decided to have the whole 5th Avenue to themselves. Well, the 5th Avenue before the real estate developers got ahold of it. And then they just fused all of the best mansions together in an absolutely delightful display of excess.

"But I wanted something singular. Something worthy of my uniqueness. I wanted to think outside the box. So I just stole the Schwab House and put it here in the middle of nowhere. Where you and I can be alone."

Then he winked at me.

Again.

He was not very good at being non-super creepy.

"Let's go back a minute and start over. What are you talking about?" I asked. "Where exactly are we? Can you explain this to me like I'm stupid? Because I am."

"We're in the House of Coventry, i.e. Archie's Realm of Destruction. Well, my Realm of Destruction. It's mine now. I'm the God of Destruction. And soon he'll be an old dried-up old useless old husk," he replied.

How did that work?

How could somebody else become a god when that god already existed?

And could a god really become an old husk?

Was I destined to be with Archie the Old Dried-Up Old Useless Old Husk???

I know Archie had told us that this sharing/transferring of powers was going on. But the technical aspects of this situation eluded me.

Then Tiziano took my hand and dragged me across the driveway, under the covered entrance, and toward the huge double doors of the house. Which swung open for him as if they were waiting for his arrival.

As he squeezed my hand tightly and pulled me into the house, I turned my head to see the figurines and Pu floating in the air, trailing behind us.

We passed through a gaudy entrance foyer that opened up into a vast main hall where a huge carpeted white marble staircase rose up from the center of the room and split into two on the second floor. Where a massive organ sat being played by tiny skulls bouncing up and down, back and forth on the keys.

"What do you think?? It's glorious, isn't it???" Tiziano questioned me, his eyes twinkling. "I think it's fitting of my stature. I mean, it doesn't have the Astor staircase. I would've rather had that in here, but I left that one where it was."

I stared at him blankly, unsure of what to say in response.

"Lina Astor fell down it, you know. Cracked her head open. Mentally incapacitated herself for the rest of her life. Isn't that *wonderful*?? That would've been lovely to walk up and down everyday, but it just doesn't go with the decor here. But this is lovely, isn't it??"

I answered him with a strained half-smile as I looked around.

Every single surface of the house—ceiling,

walls, floor, doorways, light fixtures, furniture—
everything was dripping with decoration. Nothing was left un-carved, un-gilded, unpainted, un-inlaid, un-upholstered. It was almost enough to distract me from those bouncing skulls on the organ.

"Well, *what do you think???*" Tiziano pressed me to answer.

"Why are you so concerned with my opinion?"

"Because my plan is to keep you here forever, so I want you to like it."

Huh.

Well, that wasn't what I was expecting him to say.

I gulped, loudly, and looked down at the floor.

As my heart rate markedly increased and my ears started to sweat, my kidnapper waltzed into the center of the hall and announced loudly, "I'm home, my vile servants!"

A large metal tray on two black rubbery legs entered the hall from one of several doorways on the left. It was piled high with colorful macarons.

Tiziano promptly swiped a few off the tray. He delicately placed a green one into his own mouth, while attempting to place a pink one into my mouth. Which I initially tried to fight, but he was insistent. So instead of having a cookie shoved up my nostril, I opened my mouth and started chewing.

It was delicious.

Like delicious in a way that made deliciousness delicious.

Which made me feel slightly conflicted.

Behind the two-legged tray, in the doorway it had come from, more bizarre creatures gathered to watch us. They piled up on top of each other, occasionally tumbling over as the weight proved too much. And then the piling-up process started over.

Clinging to the doorframe, twittering amongst themselves, they were sketchy little things. Seemingly composed of black lines of dust. But with legs, arms, heads, and mouths, sort of. Their eyes were empty sockets, and their round-ish shape seemed to always be shifting slightly in the breeze.

They were perhaps distant relations of recognizable animals, but their appearance was too confusing to be identifiable species. Instead they were the stuff of gouda-inspired nightmares. Not exactly terrifying, but definitely disturbing.

"What are those?" I asked Tiziano, pointing to them.

"Hmmm? Oh those? Creative thoughts. Well, destroyed creative thoughts. You know when you tell somebody about some great idea you had and then they tell you it's stupid or bad or complete doodoo and then that idea or thought gets squashed out of your brain into nothingness? Well, then that destroyed creative thought comes to live here in the Realm of Destruction. And they're particularly attracted to the God of the Realm, which is me. So there are quite a few of them here. I haven't decided if I like them or not though."

A dog entered the hall from one of the doors to the right. He was walking like a human and immediately started yelling at Tiziano with a string of profanities and references that I didn't understand.

"*What the heck have you been doing?!?!*" the dog finished.

Another dog soon followed.

"I see you've brought the next Jainkohiltzaile," the second dog said and then sighed. "What exactly do you hope to accomplish with her?

She's not even trained."

"I brought her here so you four pains in my butt could train her. You're welcome."

"Tiziano, we still need to get Sylvie out of that painting. And where is Archie?" the first dog asked.

"Lontano!!! *I am Lontano*, remember?!" he yelled, placing his hands on his hips.

"Huh? Your name is Lontano?" I asked. "I thought your name was Tiziano."

"Ha! *Tiziano?!?* Please. I'm no longer that pathetic peasant. I'm now Lontano! But again, we're getting ahead of my script! Stop talking you dogs and let me show Stella our house!"

Tiziano—I mean—Lontano grabbed my hand once again and pulled me toward the staircase, which we ascended, as he proudly explained the architectural style of the house to me.

Which I didn't understand at all.

I would at least tell you the words he was using, but I have no idea how to spell them. They seemed to be French. Maybe. Then he got to a part I could understand: 50,000 square feet, 75 rooms, pink granite floors, gym, bowling alley, three elevators. And he ended his speech by babbling about a white elephant.

Which is where he lost me again.

On the second floor landing an elderly couple sat in rocking chairs, seemingly listening to the morose organ music played by the bouncing skulls. Two normal-non-humanish dogs, and a parrot sat next to them. The woman smiled and waved at me in a friendly manner as we walked past them.

"It was their house," Lontano whispered to me as he pointed to them. "They're dead."

"What? Dead? *They're ghosts?!*" I asked.

"Yes, ghosts," he confirmed. "Oh, which reminds me. I should tell you that the ghost of your mother that you've been seeing, well, that was a phantom sent by me. Not really your mother at all. She's actually quite dead *and* unavailable, so she can't visit you. Sorry about that, pet."

"That wasn't my mother?! *Why did you do that?*"

"I had to get you to that museum somehow," he said and smiled at me. "I knew that was where it all started."

My stomach sank.

I had been tricked.

I was so stupid.

I looked pathetically back at Pu, who was still floating behind us with the figurines, and whose brow had hardened. Was he disappointed at how stupid I had been? I was.

I looked down at the floor as Lontano dragged me further into the house, down a hallway, and through a large set of glass doors onto a balcony that overlooked a titanic glassed-in courtyard full of trees, plants, and pathways.

Down a white metal spiral staircase we went, descending into the foliage. Curious little furry birds and mice-like things milling about in the undergrowth scattered as we went past. Lontano tugged me toward two gaudy plush, red sofas in the center of the courtyard. They looked completely out of place.

He tightened his grip on my hand and swung me toward one of the sofas, forcing me to quickly plant my whole body onto it, face first.

Then he stood over me and crossed his arms. Staring me down.

"Ahhhh, Stella," he cooed. "Now I'm going to have to do some serious thinking because I've already said a bunch of stuff I hadn't planned on saying yet."

Then he pushed me aside, sat down in the

center of the couch, wrapped his arm around my shoulder (yet again), and stared at me (yet again).

That situation lasted for quite a few minutes.

Minutes which I spent trying very hard not to say anything.

I just went back and forth from looking at my hands to looking at him.

He was quite good-looking.

Which was difficult to admit, since he was super creepy.

And he seemed to be a psychopath.

Every time I looked up at him he fiercely returned my gaze, smiling, winking, or doing something else equally disturbing like making a kissy face.

Then he suddenly leaned back and stared toward the ceiling.

"Stupid Tiziano," he mumbled. "Stupid boy."

He hopped up from the sofa and walked toward the other one.

As he did so, his flesh floated away into ashes, just as it had in my nightmare. Bit by bit the man disappeared from underneath his clothing and only the skeleton remained. He tilted his skull from side to side, cracking his neck. Then he snapped his boney fingers and the clothing he was wearing disappeared.

Hanging from the interior of his rib cage were eight tiny glass vials, dangling from silver chains. They glowed faint colors: pink, purples, blues, white.

He grabbed a silk robe that had magically appeared on the other sofa and put it on. And then he put his mask back on, glittered and beautiful, over his skull.

He sat down on the other sofa, his arms stretched out across the back of it, his body language oozing confidence despite him not having an actual body.

"Has anyone ever told you that your eyes are *humongous*?" he asked me.

I didn't answer him. Mostly because I already knew that I couldn't answer that type of question with any sort of dignity.

"Tiziano. Tiziano," he continued. "Was I ever really Tiziano? I was barely ever anyone...."

His words drifted off.

Silence replaced his voice.

He looked down at the floor for several minutes.

"Do you know who I am?" he then asked, seeming to restart the whole conversation like a person with dementia.

"Uhhhhh..." was all I managed to reply.

I looked at Pu, who shrugged in response.

"Let's see. There once was a very unpleasant goddess," Lontano said. "We'll call her Riot. Well, because that's generally what she went by. When she wasn't possessing dead people...."

He sighed heavily and twirled his finger in the air. Pu twirled around in the air as he did so. Which Pu clearly did not appreciate.

"She had an idea," he continued. "An idea to kill all of the lejerdemani in the world in order to prevent the next Jainkohiltzaile from being born. I went along with this idea. As she was my Master. I was a simple demi-god back then, and I didn't question the system. But I should've questioned her. Because she used my sister's soul to power this spell that makes me into what you see before you."

Then he opened up his robe and pointed to one of the tiny vial necklaces hanging off of his rib cage. The vial glowed a warm pink.

"I want you to fix this," he said.

"Uh. What's that?"

"This is my sister."

We looked at each other in silence for a moment.

"My sister is gone. And I am alone. But now, I can get her back. You simply have to break the spell that binds her inside this vial."

Simply break a spell?

Me?

I don't think so....

"Ummm. What happened to Riot?" I asked. "Why can't she break the spell if she made it?"

He laughed.

Guffawed, really.

"*Why on Earth would she break the spell she made?!?!* Plus, she's Verbena now and Verbena is a plant. She can't do anything. No, no, no. It's you and me, kid. You have to break this spell."

He clutched the vial in his skeleton hand, stood up, and lunged forward, landing next to me on my sofa.

"Now I have you!" he said, wrapping his arm back around my shoulders. "Now I have you."

He looked at me from empty eye sockets behind his mask.

"And everything will be right again. Everything will be good. Everything will be fixed. Fixed. Fixed. Fixed," he said.

He began tilting his head back and forth, while staring at me.

I tried to maintain eye contact with him.

But the whole situation was rather uncomfortable.

Especially since only one of us had eyeballs.

I glanced at Pu, still floating in the air.

He blinked at me.

Clearly, he was going to be a *great* help.

"Fixed," Lontano said again. "I want you to fix things. You fix my sister, and I'll bring those people back from these hideous figurines."

"So they *are* still alive in those?" I asked.

"Of course. How else would I use them to get you to do what I want?" he asked. "I'll still kill you, of course, well—probably—but first I'll bring those idiots back. So you can feel like your life wasn't entirely pointless. You just have to do what I tell you to do. Break the spell on my sister."

As punctuation to his ravings, he used his boney hand to claw four huge gashes into the sofa's plush flesh next to my shoulder.

He was clearly insane.

I gulped down my worry though.

"So those dogs can train me and then I can

break that spell?"

"Yes. That's what I believe. Strongly. Despite everything these turdholes keep telling me. There's always a solution."

"And if I can't break the spell? Then what happens?"

Lontano hissed at me and waved his hand toward the figurines, sending them speeding toward the ground.

"No!" I screamed, as I tried to jump up from the sofa and reach for them. But I was still stuck in place.

Luckily, he had waved again and they stopped mid-air, right before shattering on the stone floor.

I guess that was the answer to my questions.

Was I still breathing?

I watched the figurines float and spin in circles. I needed to be more careful. I needed to watch what I said.

"What will happen??" he said as he leaned toward to me, bringing his face closer to mine. "Stuff and things. Like I said, you help me. Then I'll let your family go. I'll kill you—maybe, maybe not—and we shall never speak of this again."

"Okay," I whispered.

"*Mia bella ragazza,* you're going to be so very useful to me," he said.

His masked face was now merely inches away from mine.

"This smell," he said quietly. "Yes, I remember it from Venice. I think—well—I think I missed you. Did you miss me?"

He missed me?

Did I miss him? *What? Whaaaatttt?!? Whaaaaa?!?!*

He had asked this question in a strangely sweet way, next to my ear, as he moved even closer. It was like a different person said every other word.

Stern.

Sweet.

Stern again.

Then he put his boney hand on my leg.

My back straightened and my muscles stiffened.

"You're so beautiful," he whispered.

Oh.

Poop.

Tears welled up in my eyes involuntarily.

Not now. Not now. Don't cry again. Not now.

Don't look like a total crybaby. Let's pretend to be tough here. Or at least let's pretend like psychopath skeletons tell me I'm beautiful all the time. Get it together, Stella!

I looked up. My eyes meeting his...eye sockets.

"Still. Super. Creepy," I whispered.

CHAPTER SEVENTEEN.

The Part Where I Punch Myself, But Not Really.

As Told by Morrow.

I noticed I had been holding my breath for far too long.

"How long should we stay like this?" Nora whispered.

"Talking kind of spoils the effect, Norad," Ellie said, and then sighed heavily.

We all popped out of our lawn ornaments and went over to Archie.

"*What just happened?!*" I asked him.

"A kidnapping," he answered quietly. "They're most likely going to the Realm of Destruction."

"What happened to Eagle and Penny?" Nora asked. "Are they alive? Are they all still alive in those things?"

"Yes," Archie answered. "I think so."

"*What kind of answer is that?!*" Ellie spat. "'Yes, and here's how we can save them, and make them into normal people again'—should be the type of answer you're giving us!"

"Well. 'Yes, I think so'—is the only type of answer I can give at the moment," he replied.

"If Penny's gone..." I started to say.

"She isn't gone. Well, she's gone. But she's not *gone*," Ellie brusquely interrupted me. "Right, Archie?"

"What do we need to do?" Nora interrupted her.

"Well first, can you break this cage apart and destroy it? Do you guys know how to do something like that?" he asked.

As an answer, Nora cast an 'if there's smoke, there's fire' spell on the cage, and it burnt up into ashes almost immediately.

"Thank you. I guess you guys do know how. Who exactly are you girls?" Archie asked, dusting himself off. "Penny's daughters?"

"We're Tom and Naomi Demington's kids," I explained. "So we're part Lastang and can practice magic without all that lejerdemani stuff.

Eagle's been training us, secretly."

"But we don't know everything," Ellie added. "Don't make us sound too amazing, Morrow."

"Ah, Tom? I didn't know he had children. Well, I didn't even know he could have children. But that's another thought process entirely."

"Why was everyone else paralyzed, but you were in a wooden cage?" Nora asked.

"That kind of paralysis spell wouldn't have worked on me so he put me in a Dragon Blood cage. Made from that kind of tree, which I'm allergic to. It reduces my powers tremendously. Which is why he made a Dragon Blood tree grow through the car so that I can't use it to follow him."

"You're a god, but you have *allergies*?" I asked. "That seems really lame."

"We all have our limitations, Morrow," Nora interjected. "I've never been able to figure out how to tie handle-less plastic bags closed without a twisty tie."

"I'm not sure those two things are really comparable, Norad," Ellie said.

"So if we can't use the SUV, is there another way to follow them?" I asked Archie.

"Well, does Penny have a car?" he asked.

Just then there was another shudder in the bubble.

But this time it was tremendously forceful, and it caused me to get goosebumps on my arms.

And when it was finished, we could all sense that the force field was gone.

"Sven!" Nora shouted. "He's gone!"

"I can't feel him either," Ellie said. "I mean—it. I can't feel the force field anymore."

"That's because it's gone," Archie said. "Penny and Eagle made it, and maintained it. If they leave, it stops existing. So they left the bubble."

"Which means that Penny and Eagle *were* still alive—right?! When they were transformed into the figurine? Because the force field was still in place until just now. It didn't disappear when Tiziano did his figurine-from-dusty-cloud thing. Right?" I asked.

"Either that or they were just murdered right now," Nora suggested.

We all stared at her with worried, dark expressions.

"The truth is, I've never *actually seen* Tiziano kill anyone," Archie replied. "I mean, I've never seen him do that figurine-choking spell before either. I know he's killed people. But despite him being a Demi-God of Death, *I've* never seen him kill somebody. So let's just operate under the assumption that everyone's still alive."

"You know what happens when you assume, right?" Nora asked and sighed.

"So you're sure he's killed people but you're also sure he hasn't killed these particular people," Ellie said. "Do you see how stupid that is?"

"Are we going to do something about this or just stand here debating all evening?" I asked.

"So, does Penny have a car?" Archie asked again.

"She ordered everything online and it would show up in a magic dumbwaiter in the kitchen," Ellie said.

"But she must've had a car in case of emergencies, right?" he asked.

"We didn't have any emergencies that couldn't be solved with magic," I answered.

"Well, what's in the garage?" he asked, pointing to it.

"We've never been in the garage," I said, shrugging. "It's always locked. When I was looking for stuff about magic, I didn't go in there. I wasn't looking to learn how to change spark plugs."

"Also, if you haven't noticed," Ellie added. "We're like tweens. We don't know how to drive And even if we did, we couldn't do it legally."

"That doesn't matter. I can make a car drive itself. I just need something with functioning wheels to get us there faster," Archie replied.

"So what you're saying is that we can't fly on a magic carpet?" Nora asked.

"Flying is difficult to manage if there are four of us. And flying carpets are notoriously unstable," he answered, completely serious.

"No brooms? And no magic portals?" Nora continued.

"Brooms? No one uses brooms anymore, for magic or for house cleaning. I doubt if Penny even has one. Magic portals? Well, unfortunately if you cast a transport spell to open one you can only go through it yourself. If someone other than yourself goes through your portal they often lose their memory.

"If you go through an established magic portal, one that already exists and is permanent, then no one loses their memory. Currently, however, I'm banned from my own Realm, by Tiziano. So I'll need one of you guys to open the established portal because I can't open it myself, due to that exile thing."

"So there's no magic portal here for us to use?" I asked.

"No, portals to my Realm are located in large libraries, typically. Not in the middle of a forest."

"Well, let's see if there's anything in the garage," Ellie said.

We marched over to it, and Archie cast an unspoken spell on the doors. We heard the lock mechanism snap apart and then the doors swung open.

There was indeed a car in the garage.

And it was breathtaking.

And by breathtaking I mean it took all of our breaths away with its sheer ridiculousness.

"That's horrible!" Ellie cried. "We can't possibly be seen in that thing!"

"That's amazing!" Nora exclaimed, while clapping. "I can't believe this thing has been in here this whole time and we didn't know it!"

"Is that a Victorian parlor or a car?!" Ellie asked.

"It's a 1906 Charron-Girardot-Voigt Berline de Voyage," Archie said and then exhaled forcefully. "It was Horace's car. And it'll have to do."

"No, no, *no*," Ellie said as she tried to stop him from jumping up into the driver's seat. "That thing is hideous. People will see it. I can't be seen in that. It's the first time we've left this bubble— ever—and it's in that?! No. *Just no.*"

"There's a sink and toilet in the back!!" Nora shouted as she peered through one of the parlor's windows, after jumping up onto one of the rear fenders of the massive vehicle.

"That's disgusting!!!" Ellie gasped. "I'm not— I'm not getting in that."

"You don't have to get in the toilet, Ellie. Just in the car," Nora said.

Archie had started the car's engine from the driver's seat. Which he made look far easier than it probably was. Especially since, as a cat, he couldn't even reach most of the gears and switches on this thing. Ah, the benefits of a sort-of-god's magic.

"Alright, this will work," he said. "Let's go pack some food and clothing, get Sylvie's robot, the Game of Goose die, some other stuff, and then get on the road as soon as possible."

"Shouldn't we leave immediately?!?" Nora asked, pointing toward the woods. "We have to chase down that frog!!!"

"There's no chasing down the frog, unfortunately," Archie replied. "They're already long gone. We just have to get to the House of Coventry by our own method, at our own pace."

My sisters and I gathered various supplies, and saddled ourselves with backpacks of food and clothing. Who knew how long we'd be gone for or where exactly it was we were going. There's always a neurotic need to be overly prepared when one can't possibly be prepared at all.

"Where exactly *are* we going?" Nora asked.

"The library," Archie answered.

"Uhhhh," I said. "Can you be more specific?"

"The Beinecke," he said.

"The Buy-nicky?" Nora asked.

"The Beinecke Rare Book and Manuscript Library," Archie responded. "Libraries are the repositories for knowledge about all of the things we have lost to time. They serve as gateways to the Realm of Destruction for lejerdemani. Usually I could just snap my fingers and we could go wherever I want to, but this time we'll have to follow Tiziano using the more...."

"Plebeian method?" Ellie asked.

"I wouldn't have used the word 'plebeian,'" he said and sighed.

"I don't even know what that word means..." Nora said under her breath.

"Anyway, the older the materials in the library, the better quality the gateway. So the Beinecke it is," he explained as we gathered in our house's foyer.

Then we all stared at our front door.

Ah, the front door.

The gateway out of comfort and into the unknown.

"Shotgunnnnnnn!!!!" Nora yelled as she threw open the door and ran toward the garage.

"She's not gonna give us a moment to ponder our own mortality, is she?" I said, and then sighed, deeply.

"Well, we're finally going to leave these woods. That's what you've always wanted. Right, Morrow?" Ellie asked me as we slowly followed Nora to the car.

"I don't think any of us wanted to leave Sven in this kind of situation," I replied, my eyes welling up with tears, even as I tried to fight them back.

"What's wrong with her?" Nora asked once she saw my crybaby face.

"She accidentally punched herself in the nose when we were locking the front door," Ellie replied.

I'm sure Ellie thought that explanation would help me save some face in front of Nora, but it wasn't really as helpful as she thought it was.

"I can't believe we're going to be seen in this thing. We're going to cause major catastrophes as everyone slams on their brakes at our approach," Ellie whined as we entered the garage and settled into the living room on wheels.

"Don't worry, Ellie! I'll cast an invisibility spell so no one can see us!" Nora said. "How about that?"

"In that case, I'll cast a protection spell so nobody drives into us, as they won't be able to see us if we are invisible," I added, rolling my eyes.

"That sounds good!" Archie replied. "You kids do know your stuff, huh?"

"I'd like to know the spell where we can travel back in time and punch out that Tiziano guy before he shows up at our house..." Ellie muttered.

"Well, that would open up far too many variables in the future timeline. And we still wouldn't have solved the larger issue of Sylvie being stuck in the painting. And having no way to kill Riot. But I'm sure you guys know a lot of stuff that will be useful in the future, so stay positive," Archie said, encouragingly, sort of.

"We can break a man's neck just by touching his shoulder," Nora volunteered. "And we can do that camouflage stuff. We practiced ambush spells quite a bit. We're pretty good at those idiom spells for close combat. And Eagle taught us spells for taking prisoners alive, and then torturing them for information. Oh yeah, and we can cast spells to stay awake for two weeks at a time, without food. Those are all pretty useful, right?"

Archie just stared at her for a few seconds with a feline facial expression of amazed dismay.

"Yes. Right. Well, I guess we should get going," he said as he started up the car engine.

And with that, we were off.

Out of the garage. Down the driveway. Into the woods.

And eventually out onto an actual paved road.

I was unconsciously holding my breath the whole way. Until Ellie elbowed me in the ribs because I was turning purple. The motion of the car was making me excessively queasy. I was struggling to keep it together, i.e. struggling not to toss my cookies all over this 100-year-old ancient seasickness machine.

Archie was calmly sitting in the driver's seat, not even able to see the road. Which was slightly disconcerting. He was somehow controlling the vehicle through spells and not touching anything. The car looked like it was driving itself, and knew where to go. Which was also slightly disconcerting.

Ellie and I sat in the back compartment of the vehicle. The thing was prehistoric but in excellent condition. Sitting there felt like we were about to go on a turn-of-the-century African safari. Everything was upholstered in either leather or rattan, and there were even canvas blinds you could pull down over the windows.

"What do you think the safety rating is on this thing?" I asked, half-joking, as I clutched the leather cushion I sat upon.

"I think it's the safety rating of 'don't crash into anything, ever, and you might survive,'" Ellie replied. "I just hope there aren't any bugs or mice in this mobile museum."

We zoomed out of the northern Connecticut hilly countryside, down the highway, and into New Haven. While I just made that sound like it was a super fast trip, it actually took almost an hour and that was traveling magically faster than the other cars around us.

Ellie was terrified someone would see us.

No one did.

Nora squealed with delight the whole ride, pointing out everything, and almost falling out of the car several times.

Archie sat stoically, arms crossed, at the edge of the driver's seat.

I was generally overwhelmed and my brain was fried.

Besides trying not to puke, I was worried about Penny and Eagle, and Derek and Pu, and Stella. I was worried about whether we should've left the woods. I was worried about what we were actually going to do in the Realm of Destruction once we got there.

I was worried about whether we should just continue to blindly follow Archie's plan. Do what he says. I was worried about the fact that we had no other choice. It's not like there was a lejerdemani police station where we could show up and file a complaint about the fact that our whole family had just been kidnapped by a god.

I was even worried about being too worried.

We eventually arrived at the library by driving over sidewalks, and across the middle of a campus plaza. Students walked right by us, blissfully unaware of our presence. Archie turned off the car, and jumped out.

"We're parking here?!?" I asked. "This isn't a parking lot!"

"No one can see the car anyway, except for other lejerdemani. And they won't care," Archie said as he walked toward a large light grey building that looked like a giant shipping container set up on four concrete blocks. "Just keep the invisibility spell going, Nora. We'll need it on all of us until we get through the portal."

So we got out of the car and followed him. No one noticed that we existed.

Inside the building thingy, golden light warmed the translucent stone panels of the walls that I had assumed were just solid, boring stone. And in the center of the cavernous lobby was a glass tower that rose up out of the lower floor to showcase hundreds of beautifully lit stacks of books.

"Amazing," Ellie gasped.

"It's like a golden orgy of knowledge," Nora whispered.

"How do you know that word?" Ellie asked.

"What? Golden?" Nora asked.

"I think treasure chest is a more apt phrase than orgy..." I interjected.

"Ugh, don't even say that," Archie groaned.

"What—orgy?" Nora asked.

"No. Treasure chest," Archie said and then sighed.

My sisters and I exchanged a confused glance with each other.

Then Archie sat down on the floor, started rifling through his backpack, and produced a tiny dark grey spoon-like object and a small, flat gold square plate with a circle in the center.

"Are we having soup?" I inquired sarcastically.

"Ooo! I know what that's for! *Fondue?!* Right?" Nora asked.

"This is a magnetite compass," he replied. "The ancient Chinese lejerdemani invented it for geomancy, and it's still used today to find things, or places, to foretell the future, etc."

"Geomancy?" Nora asked.

"Prognostication," Ellie replied.

Nora and I blinked at her.

"Divination," she said.

"Ooo, ooo. I know that one!" Nora confirmed.

"I'm afraid Eagle didn't use many fancy words when he explained stuff to us," I said to Archie.

"I'm pretty sure he considers us as less-than-morons."

"Also, on that note, I'm pretty sure he only explained about 0.002% of the lejerdemani world to us," Ellie added.

"That's okay. He taught you guys some things. A lot of useful things. We simply have to get him back so he can teach you the rest," he said, and smiled.

He was trying to be reassuring.

But the problem was we all knew he was trying to be reassuring.

Which then turns out to be super-non-reassuring.

I grimaced.

Ellie scratched her chin.

And Nora blew bubbles with her spit.

Archie spun the spoon on top of the gold board. It whirled around, occasionally pointing to some of the symbols etched into the plate's surface. There were about five-dozen tiny markings, but I didn't know what any of them meant. These weren't like the images on the ruined fireplace.

The spoon stopped spinning and Archie announced: "We have to go down into the basement to the staff lounge."

"Wait, wait, wait," Nora said as she held up her hand. "I think you're misinterpreting that spoon-thing. Shouldn't it be something up here in this grand main floor that opens as a portal into the Realm of Destruction? Like the glass tower in the center splits open and hundreds of books float down from it to form a giant, book-staircase that leads up into a bright, cloudy gate-way that appears in the ceiling?"

"That would be interesting," Archie said. "But I think everyone here might notice that."

He motioned to the patrons currently milling about in the library lobby, including a large campus tour group from Japan.

"The lejerdemani are usually a bit more subtle when it comes to portals to other Realms," he added.

"That's so boring," Nora whined and crossed her arms.

So we headed down into the basement level, and followed the spoon. Archie held it in front of him like a dowsing rod, and it gently vibrated in his paws whenever we would go in the proper direction.

We walked through a hallway of offices, and

Nora kept ducking into each one like a blood-hound looking for a rabbit. Touching papers on desks. Spinning in office chairs. Opening filing cabinets. Turning on computers. Turning off computers.

I clicked my tongue and glared at her when she was starting to slow us down.

"Just seeing if there's anything interesting here," she whispered to me after shrugging.

I regarded this behavior as a consequence of living ten years in a prison. I mean, bubble. And given these antics, she probably just needed to go back in and stay there.

The staff lounge was empty, luckily, as the library would soon close for the night. So Nora began opening and investigating all of the cabinets, continuing to be a nuisance to society.

Archie jumped up onto the kitchen counter and pointed to an upper cabinet.

"That's the one," he said.

"That's a cabinet," Ellie said dryly.

"Yep," he replied.

Nora scrambled up onto the counter as well, flung open the cabinet door, to reveal—700 types of coffee grounds in little plastic cups.

We looked at Archie.

"Well, behind those," he insisted.

So Nora began to fling all of the cups out of the cabinet across the lounge.

"You could do that in a *less* obvious way," Ellie complained.

But the bombardment of the carpet by coffee cups continued. And then some boxes of coffee and tea. Followed by some larger bags. And some coffee filters. Within less than a minute Nora had succeeded in emptying the cabinet.

But the back of the cabinet—was just the back of a cabinet.

Ellie scowled at Archie and put her hands on her hips.

"Well, we have to cast a spell to open it," he answered her expression. "Nora, hold your hand over the back of the cabinet and say: *Secretezza*."

She did as instructed, her body already halfway into the cabinet, and when she leaned back out, three dozen carved wooden panels appeared from out of the wall like someone had just painted them there. Each panel had a symbol on it, much like the ruined fireplace.

"Touch the torch and the book, at the same time," Archie said. "And say the word: *Cognitione*."

Before she even managed to finish saying the word, the wooden panels disappeared and she fell forward into a dark hole in the wall that sparkling dust floated out of. She crawled through and shouted back that there was another door that she was going to push open. Which she had probably already pushed open.

"It's another kitchen!" she shouted back to us.

Ellie rolled her eyes.

"So we are going into a magical Realm through a kitchen cabinet, and coming out of another kitchen cabinet?"

"These things can often be quite mundane," Archie said as he shrugged.

"Just don't fall on your clumsy butt when you come out the other side," I said, smiling at her.

She rolled her eyes at me.

So we all crawled up onto the counter, and went through the cabinet into the Realm of Destruction.

Into the House of Coventry.

Our long-lost home.

Nora was there. Playing with a pile of cloth napkins and tablecloths, which she had probably pushed out of this side's kitchen cabinet.

"At least they weren't glasses," she said after I

looked at them and blinked at her.

Ellie was there. Staring at a very handsome man in a tuxedo.

And I was there. Having been the last to come through, I had sighed at the mess Nora had made in the lounge, and then closed the cabinet door behind us.

So where was Archie?

"*Oh my shhhhhh-something I'm not allowed to say!!!*" Ellie exclaimed as she pointed at the handsome man and wiggled her whole body with some type of odd electric energy. "You're gorgeous!!!"

"Who's he?" I asked.

"That's Archie!!!" Ellie squealed. "He's a man again!"

He was indeed a man.

Dressed in a tuxedo.

Which I should've found to be weird, but for some reason I didn't.

"I noticed that, too," Nora agreed, nodding. "He came out of the cabinet that way. But I wasn't sure if I should say something. Is it polite or impolite to be like, 'Look! You aren't a cat anymore!!' to someone?"

I rolled my eyes at her.

"Uh, yes," Archie said as he dusted himself off and adjusted his outfit. "This is my typical form. Now that I'm back in my own Realm I can gain back my powers and go back to my usual appearance."

"You're hot," Ellie asserted. "Like really, really hot."

She looked at me for confirmation.

"I agree. He is attractive," I said, nodding. "But I'm not sure it's polite to comment on it so openly."

He did have a magically magnetic appearance. The kind where your eyes are automatically drawn to him. Once your gaze gets close enough it just sticks, and doesn't budge. I kept trying to not look at him but it was impossible.

"This makes all those times I wanted to pet and hold you today slightly awkward," Nora added.

"I want to pet and hold him now," Ellie whispered. "Tall, handsome. Those shoulders. That strong back. Fit. Young. 20? 21 years old? God, that face. I just want to...."

"I..." he began to interrupt her.

"He's definitely my type! So I call dibs," Ellie announced, raising her hand, and glaring at Nora and me.

"You're not even thirteen yet, Ellie. You don't have a type," I said. "And no one's calling dibs. And no one's going to be petting or holding anybody. Plus, the author said he ends up with Stella, remember?"

"I honestly preferred him as a cat," Nora said.

Ellie, Archie, and I looked at her with bewilderment.

"What? Well, anyway. Have we all forgotten why we came here?" Nora asked. "To find Penny and Eagle and everyone?"

"Oh yeah. That," Ellie said, still eyeing Archie like he was a succulent Christmas roast right out of the oven.

I was going to have to keep an eye on her.

If I could just manage to pry my own eyeballs off of Archie first.

"So where are they?" Nora prodded.

Archie stretched his neck from side to side, and stared at the ceiling. This 'kitchen' was actually just a supply room off of the actual kitchen. We seemed to be in a colonial-style tavern house with super low ceilings that I could almost reach up and touch. But Archie was definitely not really looking at the ceiling. He was staring at something that I could not see.

"They seem to be on their way to the Schwab House on Riverside," he replied. "But it's off in the woods of—upstate New York."

"You can tell that by looking at the ceiling?" I asked.

"Tiziano and I are currently sharing powers, so I can sense where he is inside my Realm. Sort of. But this also means that he knows where I am. I've just cast a spell to block our location, but I'm not sure how long that will last if he fights it."

"That's not comforting. So he can come and find us right now?" Ellie asked.

"Yes. But we can go and find him first," Archie said.

"Right. With our *super speed*," I said, dryly. "We don't even have our car anymore."

"How far away is that house from where we are right now?" Ellie asked.

"Hmmm. Not that far. But my powers aren't strong enough yet to just transport us there instantly, so we'll have to go to the basement."

"What's up with you and basements?" Nora pondered.

He tilted his head at her.

"Are any of you guys scared of heights?" he asked.

I tilted my head at him.

A basement involving heights?

None of us answered his question because we were too busy being confused by it.

"Well, anyway. Follow me," he said.

So we did.

We left the supply room and headed through the kitchen. Archie went directly to a door that led to the basement. He seemed to innately know where he was going. This must be an ability of the God of Destruction—knowing your own Realm like the back of your hand.

Then we stumbled our way down a narrow, steep staircase, and found ourselves in a dark, smelly basement with a dirt floor.

"We'll just follow these rail lines to where the streetcar can pick us up," Archie said.

Rail lines? Streetcar? *Qua???*

I saw nothing but darkness on top of darkness.

He walked ahead and a dark tunnel opened up in one of the walls as he approached it, and train tracks formed out of the darkness—running straight toward us.

"A streetcar? Under a tavern?! I was already

confused by the portal in the kitchen cabinets but now I'm *really* confused," Ellie said.

"The streetcar is—well, I established a streetcar system here in the Realm that could go anywhere and everywhere. It's not exactly the fastest form of transport, but it was meant to be more for amusement than actual use."

"*Can it go to the moon?!?!*" Nora asked.

Ellie and I shuddered with mutual, synchronized embarrassment.

"Um. No, it can't. The moon hasn't been destroyed, yet..." Archie's voice trailed off.

"Ignore her," Ellie said.

We entered the bleak tunnel. Decaying but lofty concrete columns appeared out of the darkness, standing guard on either side of us.

"Is it always like this?" I asked Archie.

"Like what?" he asked.

"Creepy. Like, it smells funny. And it's dirty. Nasty, even," I said.

I pointed to the random piles of rubble up against the columns, the posters for Rita Hayworth films that were flaking and crumbling off the walls, and the pieces of ceiling that were falling away to reveal the steel support rods.

"No, no. It's supposed to look exactly as it did

the day it was finished. The first day it was used by eager patrons," he said, and then sighed. "But Tiziano doesn't have the mental power to maintain the Realm, so what the ruins of a streetcar system look like on Earth—in the present—is seeping into this Realm."

We reached a lit subway station, probably built in the 1920s, where we waited for a streetcar to arrive.

Nora was bouncing from one foot to another.

Ellie stood with her arms crossed and her jaw locked. Probably waiting for giant sewer rats to jump out at her. She always had nightmares about those even though we lived out in the middle of the woods. It was her primary reason for instinctively disliking all cities.

And I stood very still, wondering if the streetcar was going to make me as motion-sick as the parlor-automobile.

The first sign of the streetcar's arrival was a deafening clatter, and screeching of brakes. Then one huge, bright headlight grew in the darkness.

Voices of passengers drifted down as the lead car ground to a halt in front of us, and the two drivers waved us aboard.

"They're ghosts," Archie whispered as he led us

up the stairs into the car.

Nora's eyes widened with glee.

Ellie's face went white.

And I tried not to touch anything.

"Don't worry," he added. "They can't do anything to you. They're just here to enjoy themselves."

"Oh, yeah. This place is a barrel of laughs. I'm pretty sure that tunnel's rot just gave me asthma," I complained.

But the streetcar was beautiful. I will give Archie McSunny-Pants that much credit. Everything was new and clean and almost sparkling. The whole inside and outside of the car was covered in warm wood paneling. Nothing like the hideous plastic and metal of today's subway cars that I had seen on TV.

We sat down on two wooden benches, facing each other, across the aisle from a family that looked like they were headed out for some 1940s Christmas shopping. They seemed to be discussing the order in which they should visit the downtown department stores, while giggling and pointing out illustrations of toys in a flyer.

The streetcar pulled away from the station

and rumbled through another tunnel out onto a bridge that was open on either side and looked out over a city's downtown and further out over a harbor. The children sitting next to us exclaimed and pointed out the windows, downward.

My sisters and I followed their behavior and leaned to look out the streetcar's windows, discovering that you could see straight through the wooden rails of the track down into a river, far below.

I quickly shifted in my seat so my back was firmly against the bench.

"What's that?" Nora asked as she pointed out the window.

"The river of death that tells me I am indeed scared of heights," I answered.

"No, no. Not the river. That thing," she said, continuing to point.

We strained to follow the trajectory of her finger, but eventually it was clear that she was gesturing toward a black form up ahead on the edge of the bridge. It was using an arm to hang off one of the riveted steel arches.

The creature seemed to be formed out of a mass of black, shredded strips of plastic. Like thousands of long plastic ribbons all jumbled and balled together into a person-like monster. Some of the ribbons on the edge of the creature whipped around in the wind that pushed its way around the bridge. Despite its odd format it was clear that this thing had two legs, two arms, and a head.

"Sit back and don't look at it," Archie said quickly.

We did as he instructed, but as I looked away, the creature seemed to turn its head toward us. I felt like it had seen us, even though it had no eyes.

We sat in semi-terrified silence until the streetcar lurched slightly and Archie twitched.

"Get up," he said as he jumped to his feet. "We're leaping off this thing as soon as we reach the end of this bridge."

Just then I heard creaking sounds coming from the top of the train.

"It's on the roof, isn't it?" Nora whispered.

"Yes," Archie said, pulling her to her feet, and dragging her to front of the train.

Ellie and I followed closely behind as we scrambled our way through the crowded car, up next to the driver's window by the door. The bridge ended and the streetcar entered another tunnel archway.

Archie pushed open the door and jumped out, pulling Nora with him.

I froze like a scared wimp. So Ellie pushed me out, and then leapt after me.

Yes, I closed my eyes. I'll admit that.

We all tumbled to the ground unharmed, as my protection spell from earlier was still in effect. Although that creepy monster might be able to break it. Given the chance.

As the streetcar rushed past us we saw the black creature lurching along the top of the train. And it saw us.

But then the train was gone. Off into a tunnel. Going somewhere else.

I let out a sigh of relief.

"Let's keep going," Archie insisted as he stood up, turned around and plowed ahead into another tunnel toward a staircase.

"Wait, what was that thing???" Nora asked, pulling on his sleeve.

"Come on, we have to keep moving. He'll be back here any minute," he said, hurrying his way up the stairs, with Nora still hanging on his sleeve.

So we followed him again.

Up the stairs, onto a busy street. Where Archie magically hotwired a parked car that looked about as old as that parlor thing. Then he drove us across the town, through a park, into a cemetery, which we cut across in order to drive into a forest. Where we eventually found a hidden driveway past a huge hedge. We puttered up the driveway for what seemed like forever.

"Are you sure you know where you're going?" Nora whined.

"Well, no. Not exactly. We could've taken the streetcar all the way to the house's basement, but not with that thing onboard," he answered. "But we'll get there eventually."

"Again, as Norad inquired previously, what was that thing?" Ellie asked.

"Um. You remember how Stella described the monsters that came out of the walls when she went to Penny's childhood home? It's sort of like those. A byproduct of Tiziano's insanity. The House of Coventry is home to a variety of creatures, some created by human thoughts, some created by myself as helpers.

"Some of those helpers have just carried on with their daily work, quietly waiting for the

301

time when I return and Tiziano is gone. Others have fed off of his insanity and gone insane themselves. This happens when a god becomes tainted."

"Tainted? Like spoiled?" Nora asked.

"Yes, even gods can become contaminated or polluted, and then they need to be killed and re-placed."

"Why did we have to run away from that thing?" I asked. "Do you think it's dangerous?"

"Well, given the fact that the monsters Stella encountered wanted to *eat her*, I'm guessing this guy wouldn't have wanted to throw us a party. In a Realm primarily occupied by non-corpor-eal ghosts, you demi-gods would be a very tasty meal."

My stomach dropped.

"He's most likely following us now that he's seen us, but hopefully we can stay one step ahead of him," he added.

"*Are you kidding?!*" Ellie gasped. "How are we supposed to do that??"

"Well—simply—by being one step ahead of him," Archie replied.

"Ugggghhhhhh," Nora groaned. "Thank You, Captain Obvious."

The driveway that seemed to never end did in fact end at a massive metal gate, which Archie was not able to open. He cast several spells and tried to drive the car through it, but it didn't even budge an inch.

"I bet if you were still a cat you could bounce all over this thing and hop to the other side," Nora said.

"Not helping, Norad," Ellie said.

Then she tried some spells as well. Nothing.

The three of us tried some together, nothing.

We clearly needed some special key or pass to open this thing.

"Maybe you have to be riding a giant frog to get in," Nora suggested.

"I think we'll just have to use a backdoor," Archie said, rubbing his head. "But I'm sure he'll be able to detect me making one of those. Not that he doesn't already know I'm here."

He stood over the driveway, mumbled a spell under his breath, and a piece of chalk appeared in his hand.

Then he drew a giant tic-tac-toe board on the driveway pavement.

"You're joking, right?" Ellie asked, as Nora giggled.

I just furrowed my brow, attempting to understand, but failing.

The board drew an 'X' on itself, and then Archie drew an 'O.'

This went back and forth until Archie lost.

And then it started over again.

"Don't worry, it'll eventually let me win," he said, smiling at us.

"He's cute," Ellie whispered to me. "Like super cute. But don't you feel like he's kinda stupid?"

"He *is* playing tic-tac-toe with a *driveway*, like a moron," I whispered back.

Sixty games later (I wish I was kidding), Archie finally won. And the driveway dissolved into a black hole with some stairs going down into it.

"Ooooo!!!" Nora exclaimed as she clapped her hands and started down the stairs.

"Speaking of stupid," Ellie said and clicked her tongue.

Archie followed Nora, then I went down, and Ellie brought up the rear. She may have had to push me a little bit. I really hadn't thought of myself as this much of a scaredy cat. Apparently I didn't know myself at all. Maybe I wasn't meant to exist out here in the real world.

We found ourselves in yet another basement.

This one had a train full of coal in it and several furnaces all lit and glowing. The heat was almost too much to bear.

"Let's find some stairs," Archie said, moving forward.

"Welcome home, Master," a voice murmured from a pitch-black corner as something rustled in the darkness.

"Who's there?" Archie asked as he whipped around to come face to face with the black-ribbon monster who had zoomed up next to us with unnatural speed.

Archie jumped up into the air, flipped upside down, and slipped out of the grasp of the monster. Who pursued him by shooting out long, grasping arms of hundreds of ribbons. These slammed against the walls and support columns as Archie evaded them.

But within an instant of missing him, another arm formed and shot toward Archie. He leapt and jumped around like a blurry magical ninja-thing—in a way that was surprising given his tuxedo attire. But even he would get tired eventually, right? Do gods get tired?

"He *totally* could've made it over that gate back there," Nora said. "He's like a giant flea on steroids. *He could've jumped it 7,000 times*."

"But then how would *we* have gotten over it?" I asked her.

"We coulda figured something out."

"Um. Are we going to help him?" Ellie asked. "Or just continue to pleasantly chat?"

"And how do you propose we do that?" I asked.

"Oooo. I have an idea. Hold my hand," Nora said as she grabbed my hand and motioned for Ellie to hold mine.

Then she held up her free hand in the direction of the ribbony monster of death and cast a 'cold enough to freeze the balls off a brass monkey' idiom spell. Which would be three-times as powerful since we were holding hands like toddlers on a preschool field trip.

Yes. Somehow that's how our magic worked. Like somewhere a committee got together with the agenda: 'How can we make the Demington sisters have really powerful magic that only works really powerfully in a really embarrassing way?'

And someone in that meeting said: "Let's make them hold hands every time they want to cast a really powerful spell!"

And then everyone else in the room agreed

and was like: "Heck, yeah!!! That's an excellent idea!!!"

This wasn't something any of us were proud of. Which is why I've been avoiding telling you dear readers about it. So let's just pretend that something amazing happened but it did not at all involve handholding. Okay? Okay.

Our brass monkey balls spell worked like liquid nitrogen on the creature and its rubbery parts started to slowly harden from the ground upward. Eventually making it impossible for the thing to keep growing new ribbon arms to shoot out at Archie. He was finally able to stop jumping around like a Mexican bean and catch his breath.

Once he noticed how the creature had hardened, he jumped up into the air and landed his fist on the top of its head with an unbelievably powerful punch. And the thing instantly burst apart into millions of solid rubber chunks.

Archie knelt down next to the largest pile of pieces and whispered a spell. All of the broken bits of the monster turned into sparkling dust and disappeared.

"Well," he said as he got to his feet. "If Tiziano didn't know we were here before, he does now.

Let's go upstairs and greet the bastard."

"Wow! Are you sure you should be swearing in front of three impressionable children???" Nora asked.

"I don't see any children here," he replied. "All I see are three skilled demi-gods."

"Awwww," Nora said, holding her cheeks in a fake-old-fashioned method of marking embarrassment.

I couldn't help but smile.

"Let's find some stairs," Archie said.

And so we did, with some struggling. But the basement eventually gave up its secrets.

We ascended into a kitchen the size of our whole cottage.

"Whoa!!" Nora exclaimed. "This place is gigantic!"

She began touching all of the equipment. Knives, pots, pans, etc. But Archie grabbed her by the sleeve and dragged her away. Ellie and I followed them out of the kitchen, down some hallways, around corners, up another staircase, and through a set of glass and metal doors into a room filled with trees and plants.

"So are you seeing anyone right now?" Ellie asked Archie as we stepped into this indoor paradise.

"Seeing anyone? What do you mean?" he asked.

"You know, dating anyone," she replied.

"Focus!" I said as I 'lovingly' slapped her across the shoulder. "I know this may be difficult for you to believe, but we're kind of in a life or death situation right now."

Archie ignored us—rightfully so—and started paying attention to these little furry bird things that scurried out from under the bushes and ran toward him.

He listened intently to their twittering, not afraid of them at all (unlike Ellie). Then he reached into his pocket, took something out, clasped it in his fist, and strode toward the center of this conservatory plant-room thingy.

CHAPTER EIGHTEEN.

My Twittering Hormones Are Atwitter.

But Don't Tell Anyone.

By Stella.

Strange chirping started to come from the corners of the courtyard and fill my ears. Probably from those little creatures that had hidden upon our arrival.

Pu started laughing behind his duct tape.

Lontano snapped his fingers and the two figurines vanished.

"Hey!" I yelled, as Pu growled.

"Don't worry," Lontano said. "They're in a safe place, my pet."

He stood up, looking out across the plants.

"Oh god, you *are* annoying! How did you..." he started to ask as a bright light filled the courtyard.

I instinctively closed my eyes. It was as if the sun had risen in the room. But the brightness was quickly gone like a burnt flashbulb, and the room went back to the way it had looked before.

Except now Lontano was back to his flesh and blood version, and his mask was gone. He looked like a normal man—in his bathrobe.

"*What the....?!*" he said angrily, looking down at himself.

"I prefer to talk directly to my nemesis," a man said. "Instead of a bag of bones in a Mardi Gras mask."

Lontano spat on the floor as Girolamo walked into the center of the courtyard from behind a cluster of trees.

"*You?!?!*" I gasped at Girolamo, fulfilling the cliché.

He was dressed in a tuxedo and looked very dapper. The Demington sisters were following closely behind. And all the creatures from around the courtyard swarmed toward him, but kept a respectful distance as he approached Lontano.

"*How'd you get in here?!?*" Lontano yelled.

"The basement," Girolamo replied, smiling.

Then Lontano sprang at him, ready to grab his throat.

But Girolamo dodged the attack, spun around, and punched him across the face like a boss.

Then he tossed the Game of Goose die at me while yelling: "Catch!!!"

Which—by some miracle—I did manage to catch.

And then the courtyard was gone.

Girolamo in his tux, Pu falling to the ground out of the air, and I—still on the red sofa—were now in a barren place filled with a maze of burnt tree stumps.

And with no one else around.

"Nooooo!" Girolamo moaned and grabbed his head. "*God, god, god! No!*"

"That's what I should be saying!" Pu yelled after he had ripped the duct tape off his mouth with a pained meow. "What in the world's going on here, Tuxedo Boy?!?"

"Stella, drop the die," Girolamo commanded.

I did as instructed. But the die simply fell onto the ground and we didn't change our location. I picked it up and dropped it again.

But we were still in the same place, looking at each other like a bunch of idiots.

One of whom kept picking up and dropping a die on the ground, again and again.

"Would you like to *explain* to us what's going on here, Archie?" Pu insisted as he crossed his kitty arms and pouted at Girolamo.

"*Archie?!?*" I asked, stunned. "No. This guy was Girolamo. You're telling me that *he's* the God of Destruction?!? *This is Archie?!?*"

"Yes, it is," Pu said and nodded.

"Yes, I am," Archie answered.

I didn't even know where to start.

No—I knew exactly where to start.

I knew my heart had just melted down into a hormonal puddle of goop and my stomach was burning with the fires of a thousand and one Arabian nights.

I'm supposed to end up with this person in this stupid story?!?!

How?!?

How?!?

How?!?

Archie was so good-looking that it made me feel completely on edge. Somehow his pheromones had triggered my fight or flight response. I forgot which way was up. I couldn't feel my legs. And I just kept smiling like a nutcase. Sort of in his direction, but never really making actual eye contact with him.

This man was too attractive to be human.

Of course he's not human, you moron. He's a god.

But this man is even too attractive to be a god.

Was there something more attractive than a god?

Was it okay if I grabbed him and hugged him?

What the heck was I thinking?

How do I claim him as mine?

Is it okay to pee on somebody to mark them as your territory?

What the heck is wrong with me?

"What are you thinking about Stella?" Archie asked after he had watched my facial expression change a hundred different times within the last few seconds without me actually saying anything out loud. "Did Tiziano do anything to you? Are you okay?"

"Nothing," I lied and shook my head. "I'm not thinking about anything. And he didn't really do anything to me other than tell me he's Lontano now. And he made sure to creep me the heck out.

But I'm fine, I'm fine. Everything's fine."

"You *were* thinking about something. Your screwy face is a dead give-away," Pu interjected, pointing at me accusingly. "You were totally thinking about how hot!hot!hot! Archie is as a not!not!not! cat."

"Was not," I muttered.

"Was too."

"Was not."

"Was too."

"*Was not,*" I said as I glared at Pu with a look that communicated, 'I'm going to make you eat those underwear on your head.'

He glared back and stuck his tongue out at me.

"*Anyway.* Where are we now?" Pu asked, changing topics. "And Archie, how guilty are *you* going to feel for *eternity* for having just left the Demington girls with that psychopath?"

"You don't have to rub that in," Archie replied.

What did he want rubbed in instead?

What the heck is wrong with me?

"I wanted Stella to go into the Game. I didn't think I would come, too. I mean, I wasn't touching the die. And it didn't work like that for me when I touched it, so I have no idea why it brought me here," he continued. "But don't worry too much, they're in capable hands. The Four Dogs are there."

"Let's hope they'll be okay," Pu said, scowling.

"And my Dad? Penny? Eagle?" I asked.

"They'll be fine," Archie said as he scanned the horizon, avoiding eye contact.

Right. Fine.

"Again. *Where are we?*" Pu asked.

"We should be at the game board for the Game of Goose," Archie said. "Except the board isn't here. We'll have to ask George about this so we can find Sylvie."

Then he started walking toward a large clock tower, which I hadn't noticed until then because my sofa was facing the opposite direction.

"Coming, Fatty?" Pu asked me as he started to follow Archie.

I was able to stand and walk on my own, without being physically dragged or paralyzed or carried, for the first time in what felt like a long time.

I toddled after them, staying a couple steps behind so I could watch Archie walk toward the tower.

I mean. Cough.

What the heck is wrong with me?

But wait.

I looked back at the red sofa with uneasiness.

"Can Lontano follow us here?" I asked.

"I'm not sure. I assume so," Archie said. "He's been here before, and played the Game. And he's bonded to me right now, so...."

"So he could show up at any time," Pu finished his sentence for him.

"Yes," Archie said.

Great. Just great. That's great. So great. That is made of greatness.

Also, how could I get in on this bonded to Archie action?

What the heck is wrong with me?

Focus, Stella! You've got to stay one step ahead of the crazy operatic clown.

(Maple: Welcome to the end of Book Two. You made it. Congratulations. You get a virtual hug, mug of hot cocoa, and kiss from my dog.

Maple: Also, you get to read this shameless plug for Maple's Fantastic Stories Book Three: *Damaged and Diverting*, which is now available on the planet Earth.

Maple: I'm not sure when I'll be releasing the book to other planets.

Maple: If you want to know what happens next to this weird cast of characters in this bizarre saga, be sure to read *Damaged and Diverting*.

Maple: If you want to run away screaming, it's too late. You've already been sucked in. Accept your fate. Keep reading.

Maple: Have I mentioned that the third book is called *Damaged and Diverting*? Buy it as soon as humanly possible. I need money to purchase virtual hot cocoa to distribute to all my readers.)

p.s. *Damaged and Diverting* is the third book in Maple's Fantastic Stories.

p.p.s. The third book in Maple's Fantastic Stories is *Damaged and Diverting*.

p.p.p.s. Please buy it.

www.ingramcontent.com/pod-product-compliance
Lightning Source LLC
Chambersburg PA
CBHW021942170626
46808CB00001B/7